The Pemberley Letters, vol. 1

CADY WEST

DARCY & DESIRE

A Pride & Prejudice Variation

STILLPOINT/**A**PHRODITE

Darcy & Desire: A Pride & Prejudice Variation
Published by Stillpoint/Aphrodite (stillpointdigital.com/aphrodite)
Mill Valley, California, United States of America

Copyright © 2021 by Stillpoint Digital Press

This is a work of fiction. Any resemblance to actual people, places, or events is purely coincidental. It is based on the characters, settings, and situations created by Jane Austen (1775–1817) in *Pride & Prejudice* (1813). "Elegy XIX: To His Mistress Going to Bed" by John Donne (1572–1631) was originally published in 1654. *Les Liaisons dangereuses* by Choderlos de Laclos (1741–1803) was originally published in 1782. All are in the public domain, and are used here with great love and respect for the original creators and their works.

Book designed by David Kudler and Stillpoint Digital Press
Version 1.0.0.0

Print ISBN: 978-1-938808-58-6
Ebook ISBN: 978-1-938808-59-3
Audiobook ISBN: 978-1-662204-80-7

To M,
without whom none of this would be possible
or worth doing

Contents

DARCY & DESIRE

A Pride & Prejudice Variation

Prologue – As Semele Before Jove

Pemberley, Derbyshire

"Dorry?" asked Elizabeth — but her maid had left the room, tittering stealthily.

And so he was alone with his wife as she lay in the tub — the most beautiful woman in the world, in all her unveiled glory. "No, my love," he whispered into her damp ear. "It is I." He was delighted when she squeaked and gratified when she jumped.

And then, being Lizzy Bennet, she turned to him, eyes narrowed, a slight pinkening and *eruption* of the chest the only lingering signs that he had surprised her. "Well, good." From the depths of the tub she pulled a sodden sponge and held it, streaming, out to him, her breasts — also streaming — lifting out of the water in such a way that leaving seemed suddenly impossible — as did staying. She tilted her head. "You may wash my back."

They had already shared passion that morning in their bed, and yet he found that he could not respond to such an invitation with anything less than his whole body, mind, and soul.

He closed his eyes, the sponge dripping in his hand.

Fitzwilliam Darcy knew that modesty was an attribute that few would link to his person. Yet even now, ecstatically married for nearly a month, a powerful natural reticence obliged him to avoid his own desire to gaze upon his lady wife's unclothed form, and the only name that he could possibly give that reticence was *modesty*.

She, typically, termed it *silliness*. "Open your eyes, husband. You're giving me a bath, not playing at Blind-Man's Bluff. I have not had my back well scrubbed since I left Longbourn. Florry is not here. And Jane is no longer available to do the job properly, so it is down to you."

"If you insist, my dear," Darcy said, squinting. "Lizzy, you must not laugh at me."

"Indeed, I must!" laughed Lizzy. "Your own sister has made me promise to do so no fewer than three times a day; she says that it is an efficacious tonic for your unnatural gravity. Am I so awful to look upon?"

He took a breath and answered, "You are the most beautiful sight I have ever beheld; your naked beauty threatens to destroy me, and so I close my eyes."

Lizzy blushed and smiled. "Take the sponge. Flatter me again, and you may wash the front as well."

—

Once he had further extolled her beauty — no flattery had passed his lips, since none was necessary — she had indeed allowed him to wash her front, a task to which he had committed himself most assiduously. He had so given himself to the labour, in fact, that he now found himself, clad only in a thoroughly be-sodden shirt, seated upon the edge of the large tub, his naked wife beaming catlike up at him from between his thighs. He brushed the essence of his passion from her cheek and chin. "I must go," he sighed.

"Can you leave me so?" she pouted, pressing her chest against the insides of his legs.

"Oh, Lizzy, I must."

"Cruel, cruel, heartless man! To swear love to me, and then to abandon me?" She trailed her fingers across his chest.

He took her hands and kissed those fingers. "It shall not be long."

"It shall be an *age*. I shall grow old and die. When next you see me, I shall be a shriveled old woman with hair stark grey." Though he knew that she was making sport, her eyes were overflowing, and it made his heart contract.

"It is but two weeks. You shall scarce notice that I am gone. Kitty and Georgiana shall keep you company." He kissed the inside of her wrist. "And I wish nothing more than to see you, grey-haired and handsome, and still the most beautiful woman in the world."

"Oh, Darcy, do not leave me."

"I must, my love. Starkey is waiting with the carriage. And I must go to Harrison and get him to find me new clothes."

"Are you the servant or the master?"

"I am a man who would not waste their labour or their time. And the sooner I am gone, the sooner I return."

She buried her face against his stomach, and wept.

Darcy sighed, and, though he might not have admitted it, he wept a bit himself, his tears dribbling into his wife's hair as he kissed the top of her head. "We shall write, my love. We shall write."

1 – My Dearest Darcy

From Elizabeth Darcy to Fitzwilliam Darcy

Pemberley, Derbyshire, *August 15*

My dearest Darcy –

I have ruined fully eighteen of these beautiful, creamy linen sheets to get even this far. You will laugh at me, I know, but I am in this my mother's daughter, and such prodigal waste of paper offends my sense of thrift and of propriety. And for what? Because I wish to write you, but do not know how to call you.

Dearest Husband? Too formal. *Dear Fitzwilliam?* Too familiar. *Beloved lover?* Far too familiar, though very true, and I am still close enough to what little maidenly modesty I ever possessed not to wish you to open this letter in public upon such a greeting. (And I do warn you that I cannot promise that pages to come will not venture into territory that might destroy both your modesty and what little remains of mine, and so I hope that you will save the *rest* of this letter for perusal in some private place; you may take that for a promise or for a threat, as you will!) *My own Billy?* Well, I think I can imagine the mask of mortification that *that* salutation would provoke; I will keep that one for special, private moments, I think, when you have become too much the forbidding, proud Mr. Darcy of old and I simply wish to laugh at you.

And so *My dearest Darcy* it is — not only because it strikes me as particularly euphonious, but because it is true, in whole and in parts. I love your sister — my new sister — dearly, but I can say without any compunction that you are indeed the dearest Darcy to me, dearer even than myself. You are Darcy, first and foremost — I can scarcely think of you by any other name, even though it is now my own. It is the name by which I first knew you, by which I truly came to know you, and by which I have come to love you with all of my foolish, conceited heart.

Too, you are *mine.* Pride is a sin, as we both know to our misfortune, but I think that this is one of the things of which I am proudest: that you, virtuous, accomplished, intelligent, upright — occasionally to a fault — belong to me. And that I, vain, silly, homely, and venal, belong to you, soul, mind, and body.

Of your possession of my soul you must trust. Of my mind you have this evidence — that you have been gone from our bed and from our home for but four hours, and I have had scarcely a thought but of you. Kitty and Georgiana have been attempting to engage me in some games — I hope that Kitty will indulge Georgiana's sense of play even as your sister encourages in mine some heretofore unknown vein of serious-mindedness — but I cannot be distracted from any task but of writing this, my first letter to my husband.

(Here, good my lord, is the point at which I must ask you to remember that I warned you to read this in a private place. If you failed to heed my warning, on your head be it!)

As for my body, sir, you have ample evidence of your possession of that: it has been yours to do with as it has pleased you for these past weeks and, oh, Darcy, I hope it has pleased you to take ownership so completely. It has pleased me, and pleased me again, to the point where now, having felt you within me and against me only this morning, my body *weeps* at your absence, desiring only to be taken — and to take — again.

I am a good country girl, as you know; husbandry is by no means a strange business to me. And yet I can honestly say that the mystery into which you have initiated me, the rites through which we have passed, seem as far removed from the loud exertions of cattle as any service presided over by my cousin, Mr. Collins. It is blasphemous, perhaps, to say so, but in your body and in the pleasure that it gives me, I see more evidence of God's divine grace than in any of the sermons or readings that I have witnessed — certainly in cousin's church.

Hill, our cook, used to speak at length about *fucking* and *tupping* and *servicing*, about *cocks* and *titties* and *cunts*, and we all would stand about, scandalised but fascinated. (Some, like Lydia, far too fascinated, it seems. Jane, of course, pretended not to hear, and Mary proclaimed the whole subject interesting, but only in the most abstract sense, as a reminder of the ways in which the Devil may use God's greatest gifts for his own devices.) Even so, even after many twittery, late-night whispers with Jane and with my friend Charlotte about just what it would be like to *touch* a man, to *fuck*, I can honestly say that fucking you — feeling you fuck me — is without a doubt the most astonishing and wonderful experience I have yet encountered. If there is a more astonishing experience out there over the horizon, I hope perhaps that you will not think me cowardly to say that I hope that I shall not encounter it too soon, for I am not at all certain that I should survive it.

But oh, Darcy, I want to encounter this one again. I want to encounter it soon. I want to encounter it *now*. Here I sit, writing, and I can still feel the last traces of you within me, and the sweetness of the ache that I feel, the liquid heat of your departure, of your absence, is almost beyond bearing.

But bear it I shall. For you, I could bear anything, knowing that you would do and are doing the same for me.

A queer and awesome thought has just struck me. Given our exertions of the past weeks, perhaps I *am* bearing something for you. Something that, though I know you would, you could not possibly bear for me.

Goodness. I believed that I have silenced both of us with one stroke of the pen.

It is good that I had completed the last lovely sheet of paper with my wifely musings and started on this one when I did. Georgiana and Kitty have burst in with a letter. Alas, it is not yet from you; it is from Lady Malkin, who announces that she shall be visiting this afternoon. I shall be playing the mistress of Pemberley for the very first time, it seems, and in your absence. I am determined now to dislike this woman, whom I have heard is a great beauty, for I believe she waited until she heard that you had left the county to have a look at me. Let her look all she will; if I can face your aunt, I can face anyone!

Her daughter is to come with her, and your sister, who is always the soul of discretion and generosity, as every Darcy should be — but for me, alas! — tells me that she is *quite interesting*. Knowing Georgiana as I now do, I assume this to mean that the girl is wildly odd. Her tutor, a Mr. Lackey, completes the party; him I have heard of, a poet and critic. Well, odd girls and poets are much more my fashion. I shall endure the mother for their sakes.

I shall have to sign off now and make preparation for their arrival. Or rather, I shall have to twitter about and stay out of Mrs. Reynolds's way until they come. Oh, now I wish you were here all the more!

But that were not possible: for to miss somebody more than infinitely cannot be, and so I shall sign off

Sincerely, gratefully, desperately yours,

Elizabeth Anne Bennet Darcy

PS I shall never tire of writing that name, I think. EABD

PPS Lady Malkin is very pretty. Do not look upon any ladies while you are gone, for I know that all are fairer than I, and I would not for all of the world lose your admiration so soon after gaining it. I miss you horribly. EABD

PPPS The daughter, Augustina, is indeed quite interesting. I like her far more than her mother even so. And I like the tutor as well. But I still miss you as a sparrow misses summer warmth in October. I love you, body, mind, and soul. EABD

PPPPS I shall send this now before I have second (or fifth) thoughts. My body still weeps for you. Come safely home and soon. I shall make the homecoming worth your while. EABD

2 – A Pair of Heretics

From Fitzwilliam Darcy to Elizabeth Darcy

The Rose and Thorn
Leicester, Leicestershire
August 15

My Dearest Mrs. Darcy –

Although my salutation fails to scan so prettily as yours, it is no less true, nor any less a gladness for me to be able to write than for you, I hope, to read. Alas, that you must read it, rather than hear it from my lips.

Yet without sorrow's parting, there would be no joy of reunion, and that is a felicity I greatly anticipate.

Your letter overtook me at Leicester, when I had scarce reached the inn. The arrival of a letter so soon from you at first excited my alarm, for I thought of the terrible news that arrived for you and the Gardiners at Lambton last summer — the letter I have wished so many times had never reached you, and yet which, in its own way, has led us to the blissful existence we now inhabit. In any case, my alarm was needless. Love's words, it seems, truly have wings. If it be so, than I wish that mine could carry me to you in fact as in thought, because I like you feel the same infinite loss.

It was good that you warned of what you termed your wifely musings before my hunger for you brought me to consume the letter whole. The mortification of reading such *musings* in the public room of the inn would have far surpassed that of being called "Billy" (by which name I would beg you never to address me, did I not know that begging you so would make the event all the more certain). Modesty is not, I know, a virtue much imputed to me, but yet I own this much of my bachelor modesty: that reading words of such frank intimacy in a public place would have come closer to teaching me the limits of my mortality than of my mortification.

I will ask that you read the rest of this letter in private, as I would not lose you — either to literal mortification or to mortifying embarrassment. I do not promise to be so forthright as has been your gift (from birth, if your father is to be believed), but I do promise to be no less sincere.

The ride to Leicester was uneventful, along a road that I have traveled a thousand times, and yet I was filled with a sense of newness, of seeing all as if for the first time. This caused me some wonder, until I realised that indeed I was for the first time riding that road not as Fitzwilliam Darcy, son and heir, nor as Fitzwilliam Darcy, landowner and brother, but as Fitzwilliam Darcy, husband. Though the Reverend Mr. Whitely had told us that man and wife are one flesh, I have only just realised that he meant this not merely as a metaphor for conjugal union, but as a statement of fact. I have been transformed by you. I have been born anew. Georgiana has, since our father's death, pointed out to me many, many times that I should act my age, not like an old man; I fear she shall have cause to continue berating me, for now I am a child.

Though I have always found the study of Divinity to be of greatest importance, yet I cannot say to have greatly taken any of its lessons truly to heart. A man of reason is hard pressed to see the sense in interminable lists of laws, and lines of descent, and battles, all of which belong to a world as distant as that of Homer, or of the Oriental texts that have become so fashionable of late.

Yet, as you so rightly put it, I see affirmation of God's Grace every day that I am blessed with your presence, and shall be able to survive the Purgatory of this journey only because of the promise of meeting my

Beatrice at the pinnacle on my return.

Or perhaps Beatrice was merely Dante's Elizabeth, for I cannot believe that his love was any more a beacon than my own. Therefore I hold you to be the true original, and Mr. Alighieri's muse merely a reflection.

My, what a pair of heretics we are, Lizzy. Yet I would not recant this theology for all of the Rev. Mr. Whitleys or Mr. Collinses in Christendom.

That you might be bearing something for me that while, as you say, I would, I cannot bear for you — *that* was something the rendered me more than speechless on the very first night that we enjoyed together. You had fallen asleep, and I lay there, with my head upon your belly, gazing up at your naked perfection — feeling my old self destroyed as Semele before Jove — and it occurred to me that beneath my cheek there might have been a spark struck by our passion. I wept, Lizzy, for the reality of what it might mean to have a child with you was truly an awesome and an awful realization. I had thought that I knew what it would mean. I was wrong. I know now that I still do not *conceive*, as you may indeed already have done. I hope that you will not think me cowardly to say that the realization struck me so to the core that I hope the reality is some time off — I am not sure that I should survive it.

Too, I would not wish to stop *trying* to conceive any time soon, the trying being so astonishing an adventure that I never wish to reach its end — unlike my current journey.

~~Oh, Lizzy, I~~
~~Elizabeth, you are~~
~~Thy breasts are like unto~~
I am a coward, it is true.

I have seated myself here, ready to tell you — as you have so movingly told me (and you have moved both my soul and my body, please believe me) — how you have initiated me into a mystery beyond measure. And yet, though this is true, and though I have found with you a realm of experience previously unknown to me, you know that I have experienced carnal embrace before I met you.

That strikes me as a particularly ugly and ridiculous phrase, "carnal embrace." Very well, then, I shall follow your example, calling the act by its proper English name, and say that it saddens me that I fucked any woman before you and I fucked.

I am not proud that it is so, but as I have already admitted the fault, so it is. I am not like some men who are pleased to indulge a sin in themselves that they condemn in women. Even so, in this I can scarcely even condemn myself, but for the fact that my weakness robbed me of a shared experience with the woman I love.

The reason that I tell you so much is that the woman who first shared with me the embrace that should have been yours was, in fact, none other than Lady Malkin.

I was not as old as my sister is now, and she was a married woman of about your years and already a mother. She was, as you say, very pretty (though not as beautiful as you) and very forceful in pursuing her will, which was myself. I thought at the time that she desired me for my own virtues; indeed, she made me believe that I was the only man to know her intimately — ah, another euphemism! — the only man to fuck her but her husband, whom she claimed to have shared a bed with only once. Knowing her as I came to do, I cannot in good conscience give credence to those assertions. I believe now that she merely wished to indulge her own pleasure, and to prepare for the eventuality of Lord Malkin's death. An alliance between my family and hers would have appealed to her, as it would, even, to my father, who counted Lord Malkin as a close friend. Be that as it may, I wish — for Lord Malkin's sake, for their children's, and for Lady Malkin's — that his departure might be many, many years in the future.

In the end, she dallied with me — fucked me — on four occasions, each less a pleasure to me than the last, for with each encounter, she lost interest (being intrigued, I believe, more by acquiring what she could not have than by having it), and I felt my own impropriety more and more deeply. On the day of what was to have been our fifth assignation, having made up my mind to see her no more, I arrived early to the stable where we were wont to meet, and there found her engaged with another young man in very much the same sorts of embraces — fucking — that she had shared with me. The young man was, you will not perhaps be surprised to know, George Wickham. I can blame him in this even less than I blame myself — given the difference in their stations, how was he to have evaded the trap of her allurements without giving offense? Of course, I suspect now that it never occurred to him to try.

From that day to this, I have not spoken privately to Lady Malkin, nor to her husband. Lord Malkin I have not met except in company because of my own shame at having abused his honour. Her I have refused to see because I could not think how to speak to such a women after such an experience.

Young Thomas and Augustina have been welcome at Pemberley, and Georgiana has been a frequent visitor at Langley Park. Indeed, Lord Malkin has written me on several occasions suggesting an union between his son and my sister. Georgiana, however, has made it clear that, much as she enjoys the *quite interesting* Augustina, Thomas is not for her, and so I have been spared the mortification of *that* alliance, at least.

I should not have been shocked, then, that Lady Malkin swooped in the moment that she heard that you were at Pemberley unattended.

Please, beloved, forgive me. I should have thought that she would engage in such a stratagem. I should at the very least have warned you. I do not believe the lady to be evil, yet I cannot think of her as anything but vicious. *Venal* you may have called yourself, but even now you are the model of chastity against which all women must be measured, and against which standard I fear to say that Lady Malkin fails most miserably.

It is pointless for me to say that what I knew with her is nothing to what you have shown me. That would be to compare the murky light of a guttering candle to the full brilliance of the Sun. I know too that even to say such a thing would do nothing to alleviate your just anger with me.

Please believe that I am always

Desperately, eternally, completely
Yours,

Fitzwilliam Henry, Darcy by birth
(Bennet by God's good Grace)

PS I give you leave to shoot Lady Malkin if she misbehaves. My being a Justice of the Peace for the county must be of some utility, must it not? — FHD(B)

PPS I am a ship tossed at sea, no sight of the land I long to return to, beset on all sides, and yet aware only of the desire to dock myself in your safe harbor once more. I miss you more than my soul or body can stand. But I shall have to satisfy myself with dreams of you, and will seal this, for if I keep thinking of you, I shall never sleep, but be scuttled by my own desire for you. I long for you, Lizzy. I live to hear from you. — FHD(B)

PPPS I am ashamed that it took no more than rereading your "wifely musings" to render me utterly ready for your presence, to desire that I might show you even now how truly penitent I am and how fully I wish to make amends. Alas, the only embrace I have to satisfy the need you inspire is mine own, and so I must satisfy myself with that, as you have already inspired me to do twice since your letter arrived. Another sin on my side of the ledger, but one I could no more abstain from after these last weeks of bliss than I could from breathing. Nor do I count it a sin to give myself relief while thinking on the perfection of my wife, whom I dream to see, to touch, and, yes, to *fuck* every waking moment. More blasphemy. I shall truly seal this now and send it or I shall begin to tell you just how I dream. — FHD(B)

3 – The Memory of Your Presence

From Elizabeth Darcy to Fitzwilliam Darcy

Pemberley, Derbyshire, *August 16*

My dearest Darcy,

Well, then, when *shall* I hear just how you dream? My curiosity presses so determined a campaign against my patience that my propriety has completely fled the field. Oh, Darcy, do tell me these dreams. I *long* to hear them. And if you begin to tell me yours, perhaps I shall do my wifely duty and tell you mine own.

I shall give the gamekeeper (is his name truly Grouse?) permission to shoot Lady Malkin on sight. I shall ask him to aim for her lovely head, however, since her gown was too pretty to be spoiled. After their visit yesterday, Kitty engaged Georgiana in nearly an half an hour's speculation on whether the lace at the lady's sleeves were Chantilly (and whether it would have looked as good with their dark hair as with Lady Malkin's fair), while Georgiana managed to get Kitty to talk for a good fifteen minutes about the progress of the war and the propriety of purchasing goods from an enemy nation. I believe my project in encouraging my sister's seriousness and your sister's silliness is, so far, to be rated a success.

Darcy, I am so sorry that she robbed you of an experience that I can assure you was well worth the wait. I have known boys of Georgiana's age

— though none as beautiful and virtuous as I am assured you were when Lady M stole your virginity. I can with certainty affirm two things about them: of the first, that they are barely in control of their feet or their tongues, let alone their actions; and of the second, that a grown woman who finds fucking such puppies appealing (I was about to say "dallying with such boys," but knew you would be disappointed at my stooping to euphemism) is a woman of very peculiar desires indeed, her infidelity notwithstanding. That she chose to fuck young George Wickham is a further damning piece of evidence toward this argument.

Other than daydreams of killing her with a birding gun, I have found my thoughts since your letter arrived this morning have circled around you, sweet, pretty, and serious as I am sure you were, and how I wish that I had been the one to initiate you into the mystery we now share. And yet if I were to encounter the boy Fitzwilliam (son and heir) as I am now, my love and desire would be protective and maternal rather than wifely, while if we had met at the time I should have been a scabby-kneed little hellion, more interested in playing Tom-o'-Straw with you than games of the sort we have enjoyed together so recently.

Oh, and now that I write that, Darcy, I feel the pang of wanting to play those games with you again wash through me like the rain that is even now pouring across the grounds at Pemberley. Oh, Darcy, my dearest Darcy, I woke this morning in our bed, alone. Alone! And my body felt that solitude, felt your absence, even more deeply than it did when you left me, bereft, yesterday. For this this morning I had only the dream and the memory of your presence beside and within me, while yesterday I had the very real, very physical reminder of our passion — of our *fucking* — to still the ache, this morning I had only the dream of the memory, or perhaps the memory of the dream, since I woke with the immediate sense of your pressing within me. Alas, that it was but dream of you, of your body and your presence. And yet, for these next days and nights, it is what I shall have to warm and comfort me.

I do, however, also warm myself with that dream — and with the very concrete possibility that there is in fact a part of you growing within me. Oh, that dream, that thought makes me warm, Darcy, and in more ways than one. I find that that — conceiving of conceiving, if you will — strikes me (even me!) quite dumb, and not altogether in a bad way, but as you say, in a way that makes me hope, perhaps, that I have not fully re-alised the concept (of conception), and that, perhaps, we may take a great deal more time *"trying* to conceive," since, like you, I find the attempt itself "so astonishing an adventure."

And I am glad, my dearest Darcy, that you feel as I do. Because if it were only I, I know that I should be utterly lost: your slave, to do with as you please. As I am, in any case, since I wish you to do as you please with me, and do so often. And do so again *soon,* though I know it cannot be.

I find that I must stop myself from beginning every other sentence, "I miss you" or "I desire you" or, if I am to be as forthright as you seem to think me, "I want you to fuck me." I beg your pardon, my love, since it seems that, for all her pride, your wife is nothing more than a love-sick girl. Oh, when I think of how dismissive I have been of my sisters and their infatuations! Yet here I am — as speechless as Jane, as silly as Kitty, and as unbridled in my desires as Lydia. Oh, were Mary only here to comfort me with her chaste discipline! She could read some of cousin Collins's sermons, which I have no doubt would cool my fever consid-erably. Yet I have no wish to have that fever cooled. I know the physic that will break it, and the dark-haired, dark-eyed man who could alone administer it rides away from me, rather than *riding me,* and he leaves me green and moist and ready for his return. I am sure that is not a pretty image for you to contemplate. Ah, me — for, like you, the only embrace I have to satisfy the desire that you have engendered in me is mine own.

It is kind of you to term me "a model of chastity" — yet I promise you, my lord and husband, my thoughts this morning have been any-thing but chaste.

Your letter arrived not long after I first stirred, but before I had left my bed. Young Florry brought it in, all a-twitter, since the post-boy had delivered it to Mr. Reynolds, the butler, with the very particular instruc-tions that it be delivered into my hand (and my hand only) at the earliest convenience. I believe our correspondence has already given the servants some cause to gossip, and yet I cannot find it in myself to be ashamed. I am pleased that they know how I love you, and proud that they should know that you love me. As Florry burst in, however, I had only just fin-ished *embracing myself* in your memory, a brief satisfaction that only left me the more hungry. I was glad, then, that she did not open the drapes before she had deposited the infamous letter beside me on the bed, for I had time both to compose myself — and to close my gown. I may be proud that they know your effect upon me, yet I would not have them see it!

I had to ask Florry to leave me to my private to read your letter — I had to ask her three times.

I do not think I am yet used to having people whose labour it is to take care of me. I have seen to that work almost entirely on my own since Lydia's birth — with some help from Jane, of course — and so I have not yet become used to delegating that duty to another. I like Florry a great deal. She is sweet and funny, and reminds me a bit of Charlotte as a young girl, and so I know that I shall come to adore her as a maid and companion.

Yet it goes, perhaps, without saying that it was not for her care or companionship that I wished when she burst in to our chamber and the big, half-empty bed we have made such good use of over the past weeks.

It was, then, a delight — once I had shooed her out the door — to open your letter and read your dear, sweet, *modest*, and *less than perfectly correct* words! Oh, my dearest, naughtiest Darcy, I am pleased and proud once more, to have inspired you — you! — to write with something like the passion that I have enjoyed with you in that self-same bed. I consider it once of my greatest accomplishments, though not one I would share with the world.

And my heart aches that you feel such regret for an act for which I neither blame nor condemn you. You are as I would wish you to be. You are perfect, and — our American cousins notwithstanding — I do not believe that it is possible to make anything "more perfect." Your experiences — all of them, including those with Lady Malkin and Wickham and your aunt and even our sister-in-law Caroline — all of them have made you the man whom I have grown to love with all of my giddy, frivolous, un-chaste heart. Do not regret anything that has brought us to this place, I beg of you, Darcy, for I would not change you one iota for all the world.

Well, I have dallied here in our room for most of the morning, writing this, my *second* letter to you. And at the least I have this time had to tear up only two pieces of paper (which I should burn, now that I think on it, because I would not have Florry or anyone else read my girlish ramblings — anyone else but you, of course!) What a slugabed Mrs. Reynolds must think me. I shall blot my pages once again, while the skies seem to have cleared somewhat, and see if love's swift wings can carry my words to you and yours to me just as swiftly, for without you I am nothing.

Wistfully, madly, longingly yours,

Elizabeth Anne Bennet Darcy

PS It continues to fill me with joy and wonder to be able to write that name. And you calling yourself a "Bennet by God's good Grace" makes my full measure of delight overflow completely. — EABD

PPS I walked into the library, seeking Mr. Reynolds to post this letter, and found our sisters, both looking very serious. Georgiana was playing on the pianoforte — something very playful and oriental-sounding — while Kitty was reading in French. My sister Catherine has few accomplishments aside from gossip and a fine eye for lace, however alone of all of us, she managed to acquire from our father a skill at foreign tongues. Or at least *one* foreign tongue. And I am certain that her interest had more to do with some of the less decorous titles in Father's library. In any case, as I walked into the room, Kitty stopped reading and folded the book upon her lap — face down — with such studied innocence as I have seen her use all too often. Georgiana, on the other hand, blushed very prettily, but continued to play with nary a note missed. I fear that my project with our sisters may not be going as well as I had hoped. — EABD

PPPS I quite like it when *your* full measure of delight overflows completely. (I love it all the more so when it overflows inside of me.) — EABD

PPPPS Consternation. Lady Malkin has written again. It was too much to hope either that she would simply send a letter of thanks for having invited herself to our home yesterday, or would trespass again and allow us to shoot her once and for all. No. She has invited me, Georgiana, and Kitty to Langley Park this evening, in order to meet the poet Mr. Shelley, who is apparently an acquaintance of Mr. Lackey the tutor, and who will read some of his poems. I cannot suppose that it would be considered good manners to bring a pistol to a poetry reading, though perhaps gunplay might improve my opinion of Mr. Shelley's poetry. Consternation. I am beset. I am to be in company again, and not the company for which I long. — EABD

PPPPPS WHEN ARE YOU TO COME HOME? HAS IT NOT ALREADY BEEN PAST A MONTH? — EABD

4 – My Dreams of You

From Fitzwilliam Darcy to Elizabeth Darcy

My Dearest Mrs. Darcy,

Your letter overtook me sooner than I might have hoped, since to-day's rain has caused the River Nene, which I have never known to be anything but mild in summer, to rise into a torrent that threatened to wash away the bridge. I cursed at the delay, and yet, upon returning to the town, found that the post-coach and your letter had reached Northampton and were awaiting me.

No, my love, it has not been a month, nor yet a week, though I too feel the hours and days stretch out cruelly before me. As I write it has been some thirty-three hours. And fourteen minutes. And I promise to be back by your side long before this month has waned. That is a promise to you and to myself that I would rather die than fail to keep.

Yes, the gamekeeper is indeed named Grouse. The Grouses have been custodians of the Pemberley woods since time immemorial — they are named in the Domesday Book, I am told — and so my father gave me to understand that, while the county may believe that the Grouses serve the estate, the Fitzwilliamses and the Darcys have always known that we live on this land at the sufferance of the Grouses. "Young" Grouse, the current gamekeeper, knows every tree and animal on the estate (by name, I would swear), and any with which he might not have a personal acquaintance are certainly known to his father, "Old" Grouse, who is sadly now blind, but can still tell a gripping tale of poachers routed and fox kits saved. Both Georgiana and I were nursed by Mistress Grouse (wife of Grouse the Elder). And young Florence, your lady's maid, is Grouse the Younger's niece. The Grouses are, on the whole, little impressed with station or with frippery, and so I am sure that Grouse would be happy to put down the trespasser for you. And I know that he is a fine enough shot that you ought to be able to mount the lady's pretty gown upon the wall unblemished, Chantilly lace and all.

It is entirely typical of your kindness to acquit me of a fault for which I cannot forgive myself. I know that you mean to free me of the sin of my unfortunate liaison. Yet guilt I feel, and your forgiveness does not wash away the stain. Indeed, I am afraid that I feel the guilt all the more deeply for your acquittal, though, as I say, I cannot tell you why. The Darcys have been good members of the United Church since the Reformation, yet I apparently retain enough of my ancestors' Catholicism to feel the need for more than forgiveness. What that *more* might be I do not know and cannot say. I cannot even beg your forgiveness, since you have already given it freely.

I fear that this letter will come too late for me to dissuade you from visiting Langley Park. Lady Malkin is a very [SCRATCHED OUT] I fear too that I am far too late to warn you that Georgiana holds Mr. Wordsworth (and by extension Mr. Shelley) in high esteem, and that you might treat their poetry with more respect than, perhaps, you may yourself feel. I am not a great reader of the modern poets — I have always had a greater regard for the poetry of Donne and, of course, Shakespeare than of Dryden or Pope or any of the latter-day poetasters. (Milton I have always felt that I *should* like, though the liking has never equaled the desire, and I have never been certain why I do not enjoy him more.) And of course I have always greatly enjoyed the poems of Catullus, Horace, Sappho, and Homer. Which, may I venture to assume, since you claim no skill in tongues, you have not read in the original? If so, have I found at last the one way in which Elizabeth Bennet is anything less than absolutely perfect?

Your project with Georgiana and Kitty is an admirable one, and I will say that it seems that it is proceeding well. For your sister Catherine, while I will grant that any increasing of her seriousness would perhaps be a good thing, I find that her playfulness is a pleasant addition to our household. And particularly, any encouragement she might give Georgiana in engaging in games and fun must be deemed good. I fear that my own perverse solemnity has dampened any playful spirit my sister may have had — and the events at Ramsgate two summers ago caused her to question her own discernment. I have assured her that, while that discernment was indeed in error in that case, one mistake (however grave the consequences may have been) should not cause her to lose all faith in herself, yet has she deferred to my judgment entirely these past years. There was a time when she was wont to tease me constantly, a habit that at the time I did not appreciate; she has only begun to do so again since your arrival in the family — I cannot think what inspired her to indulge her disrespectful side once more. In earlier days, I might not have welcomed disobedience or disrespect from my sister and ward, even of the mildest variety, and yet I now see how badly her spirit has been diminished, and welcome its return.

As for the presence of what you term "less decorous" volumes in the Pemberley library, particularly in French, I freely admit that our family has always felt it wise to include on our shelves some few books that may fall somewhat outside of the bounds of polite expression. After all, how may one learn what is correct without seeing what is incorrect? As to the French collection, it was greatly expanded when a distant cousin, the elderly Chevalier Danceny, arrived at Pemberley some twenty years ago, flying *La Terreur* in Paris, bearing nothing but the silk clothes on his back and a trunkful of recherché novels. Some of the most outlandish volumes my father insisted (after the chevalier's death some few years later) be stored on the very top shelves, which cannot be reached without a gardening ladder, far from the prying eyes of impressionable sons (and daughters). However, he read some few of them (as have I), and so some of them may have found their way to lower shelves, within the reach of curious sisters. Should the volume be one of those… Well, if you were able to discover the author of the volume that caused Kitty and Georgiana such excitement, I might advise you whether to abjure them from reading further, and how we may give their reading some greater understanding of its subject matter and circumstances. For most of the volumes, I am sure that the worst that we can fear is titillation. For some few — well, for those I fear we may need to teach our sisters how to understand actions and tastes that I am not certain that I understand fully myself, and while I know you to be of the broadest possible mind, I am not certain that they fall within your ken any more than they do mine.

And as for my dreams of you, I will do my best to tell you, though my own unease and lack of utter forthrightness may decrease your appreciation of them. If so, please let me assure you, they are dreams — waking and sleeping — of such delight as ravish my senses almost as thoroughly as you do yourself. When I wrote last night, I had been *embracing myself* to the memory of your having wakened me yesterday morning — of your naked form, the banner of such wonders as you have bestowed and of those yet promised — of your taking my member, first in your hand, fine and firm, and then within your mouth, moist and warm — oh, Lizzy, the feeling of your tongue and lips upon me, of those eloquent, extraordinary organs — you played upon me like the most talented of flautists and made my whole body *sing*

And you have now made it sing again, as you did last night. I have *embraced myself* once more, and though I, like you, am distraught that the only embrace I have to relieve my desire for you is my own, yet I could not forebear touching myself so, not when my body longs so desperately for the relief only you can give.

I have spilt upon my trousers. I know that my valet Harrison would never mention seeing such a stain, and yet I know too that he *will* see it, and will know its cause. I am curious, however, because while I might have felt completely abashed at knowing such a thing a year ago, now, while I am somewhat embarrassed (and annoyed at causing needless labour), I feel no shame whatsoever, for I know that he will understand, as I do, what inspired me to my *measure of delight overflowing* in so fulsome a manner. And neither do I feel any shame in admitting that I too quite enjoy it overflowing *within you*. And even out of you. I long to kiss, as I did yesterday, the overflow from you lips.

Ah. You have inspired another ecstasy. And I have made another mess. Oh, my love, how shall we survive this separation? I feel as incapable of forgoing the delights that we have shared as an opium eater his poppy milk. All of my favourite parts of you appear to my imagination, and from thence to my senses, and then I am lost.

They have promised that, tomorrow, should the bridge be yet closed, the old ferry shall take us across the swollen Nene. I hope to reach London by nightfall, and will speak to my factor and to your uncle Gardiner as soon as may be accomplished. There is much business for me to address while I am in the city, yet I find that I cannot abide the idea of staying there any longer than is absolutely necessary. A siren calls me home, and my Penelope awaits. I cannot bear to make her wait too long.

Utterly, unrestrainedly, everlastingly,
Yours,

Fitzwilliam Henry, Darcy by birth
(Bennet by God's good Grace)

PS I believe that I prefer to think of you as my Penelope rather than my Beatrice, for while Dante could only unite with his beloved in the most chaste and religious of senses, Penelope was Ulysses' wife, and I have no doubt that their union (or rather re-union) shook their living tree-bed to its roots and their island home to its core. — FHD(B)

PPS As I understand it, the very first of God's commandments is "Be fruitful and multiply." One flesh as we are, I believe, then, that for us to *fuck*, to unite in body as in spirit, to abandon ourself to each other completely and without reservation, is the most religious of endeavours, and so, in the eyes of those churchmen that both you and I have spoken of so dismissively and irreligiously of late, considered *chaste*. Let no man — or woman — call my Elizabeth *anything* but the model of chastity, even when I *ride her* until she screams, and screams again. — FHD(B)

PPPS We are each slave to the other. I would have it no other way. Would you? — FHD(B)

PPPPS I should like to watch you embrace yourself. — FHD(B)

PPPPPS I will see if a mail coach may be found going north that might bring this to you overnight. I dream that it shall reach you once again in bed, and that my ecstasies (however haltingly described) might inspire the same in you. I miss you, my dearest Mrs. Darcy. I long for you. My body aches for you. My kiss for you is upon this paper — would that I could seal it with a stronger sign of passion — but a kiss must suffice. — FHD(B)

5 – Let All of England Know

From Elizabeth Darcy to Fitzwilliam Darcy

Pemberley, Derbyshire, *August 16/17*

My dearest Darcy,

I am beginning this letter the night of my sending the last. I do not know whether my most recent plea has even reached you yet, or whether it will trail after you across the south of England like a dog seeking its master. Yet we have had so remarkable a day, and my soul (and body) feel your absence so keenly, that I can think of nothing to do but write to you.

On the coach ride to Langley Park this afternoon, Georgiana and I had an ardent discussion on the subject of poetry. Even Kitty joined in — on Georgiana's side. (Kitty, in the manner of the Bennets, has shortened your sister's name and taken to calling her *Gigi*. I am uncertain how to feel about this, though Georgiana herself seems to delight in the nickname. If you feel it is too indecorous, I shall dissuade Kitty. Otherwise, I shall let them call each other what they will.)

I made what I now perceive to be the mistake of mentioning my lack of admiration for Mr. Shelley's verses and for Lord Byron's. Georgiana — who has always been so respectful, loving, and deferential toward me — answered me with unforeseen passion, telling me that she believed that the lines of Mr. Shelley and Lord Byron and some of the other modern poets harken back to what she termed the "virile prosody" of Shakespeare and some of his contemporaries. (I will grant that Kitty found the phrase "virile prosody" wildly humorous. Yet I believe that this was a point upon which she felt that she could agree. I know that both she and Lydia delighted in reading some of the less *polite* passages in Shakespeare's plays and poems. As, I must admit, did Jane and I, and even, on some occasions, Mary, who was particularly enamored of *The Rape of Lucrece. Virile prosody,* indeed!)

In any case, I granted to Georgiana that the English poems of the past few centuries have become more and more *artful,* even as they have become less and less *artistic* — that they have mostly seemed to be intended to display their own cleverness, rather than communicating the beauty of their subjects and the passions of their authors. And I granted, too, that some few recent poets have dispensed with a certain sheen of artifice while displaying the true genius of art. Yet, for me, I told our sisters that while I admire the lines of Lord Byron and Mssrs. Shelley and Wordsworth, I prefer the writing of Mr. Coleridge and of my father's great favourite, the *quite interesting* Mr. Blake, precisely for the *virility* of their *prosody.* Georgiana riposted, reciting one of Shelley's poems from memory — but before I had an opportunity to share my own thoughts, we arrived at Langley Park, and Kitty and I were both struck dumb by the artless artfulness of the gardens as we approached the house. I dearly love the grounds of Pemberley — quite the most beautiful estate I have ever seen — and am proud call them home. Yet the gardens about the Malkin manor are precisely the embodiment of what I had been attempting to describe in poetry: a masterwork of artifice turned toward appearing completely natural — the perfection of nature as art. I do not know that I could live in such a place — it would feel like living in a particularly perfect, particularly unearthly painting, I think — but I could not fail to appreciate the beauty of the landscape.

Augustina and the heretofore unmet Thomas greeted us at the drive, Augustina embracing Kitty and Georgiana warmly (though awkwardly, as she seems to do everything). They led us through a long hall full of paintings of redheaded, haughty Malkins — a much less welcoming horde than those dark Darcys who gaze down from the walls at Pemberley. Augustina and our sisters tittered and giggled the whole way, while young Thomas kept me silent company, glancing surreptitiously at the girls.

They led us to a sitting room that was clearly designed to make the greatest possible use of the lovely gardens, opening out toward a lake and fountain that look almost *too* natural. There we met the woman who has quickly become my fair, flaxen-haired Nemesis in Derbyshire, Lady Malkin, who was holding court over a small gathering: Mr. Lackey, a man whom I immediately recognised (from his famous torrent of hair) as Mr. Shelley, and a young, rather serious looking girl who was introduced to us as Mary. They were, as we arrived, discussing the number of trout in the lake, a subject about which I would not have surmised that any of them were interested, but as soon as we had been introduced, Augustina began to hold forth with great passion about how such populations follow mathematical formulae, complex patterns of increase and decrease that interact with *other* formulae — rainfall patterns, the numbers of insects for the fish to eat and of otters and other animals to eat them — to create what seems to be a completely random number of fish in the lake, yet which obey, in fact, very clear rules. (Clear, Mr. Lackey pointed out, only if you had God's omniscient view of every ant's step and every tempest's sweep.) By this point, only Mr. Lackey, Georgiana and I were listening — oh, and the young girl Mary, whose dark eyes were fixed upon Augustina. My sister was batting her eyelashes at young Mr. Giniver, while his mother and Mr. Shelley were whispering about *something*.

I must tell you, Darcy, that while I could not understand all or even many of the points that Augustina and her tutor were arguing, I nonetheless had a momentary sense of glimpsing something grand — the secret machinery of the Prime Mover at work, perhaps? Augustina is a quite, *quite interesting* young woman indeed.

When Augustina saw that she had predominated the conversation, she apologised, blushing and twitching. Georgiana and I assured her that she need not apologise, that we had been much interested in her thoughts. Mary (whose surname I failed to ascertain) said with great solemnity that Augustina was very pretty when she was excited. The whole room laughed, causing Augustina to blush and twitch even more, at which point Lady Malkin announced that, her daughter "having ridden her hobbyhorse to death," perhaps Mr. Shelley would be willing to share one of his poems.

The girls all clapped, as did I, though more for Georgiana's sake than my own, and Mr. Shelley took a notebook from Mary, informing us that this was a poem that he had only just begun to work on, a kind of philosophical fairytale, and, turning to the lady of the house, launched into a long and — if I may be entirely frank — not terribly virile exploration in verse on the subjects (I believe) of Death and Sleep and the ills of modern society. The poet and the poem rambled on for some time. There was much talk of wandering, and of souls, of ghosts and such. The younger girls seemed quite captivated. Thomas and I, alas, were less so. Lady Malkin, to whom Mr. Shelley addressed the whole of the interminable poem, seemed to be listening, not the poet's words, but to his thoughts. Or perhaps his desires.

At some point, a ghostly figure entered the verses, a hermit of some sort, and Lady Malkin interrupted to say that the new garden included a hermitage, very picturesquely gloomy, on the opposite shore of the lake. It was, she informed him regretfully, unoccupied.

As if he had not just been holding forth in verse for more than an hour — as if this were merely some conversation between the two of them — the poet demanded that she show him this curiosity immediately, and they left through the large, glass doors, while the rest of us sat, somewhat startled, and watched as they began to promenade about the small lake.

I do not know what the others thought — I would not presume to ask them — but it was clear to me that we were watching the prelude to an assignation. And I found myself astonished at the audacity. If I had not already taken an immediate and strong dislike to the woman, if you had not already provided me with more reasons for my prejudice, and if she had not earlier dismissed her own daughter so appallingly, I must say that I would, even so, have conceived in that moment of a thorough abhorrence of Lady Malkin. I am afraid that I must agree with you when you allowed that she is far from the model of chastity, however I may stand.

After we had all sat, uncertain how to fill the silence, I turned to Mr. Lackey, who seemed the least discomposed of us, and asked him whether the striking garden had been planted recently. He informed me that, yes, it had been renovated the previous year. Kitty then asked young Thomas whether there were any good hunting or fishing in the park, which he assured her there was, and conversation was rekindled about the room, all of us speaking with more than common vivacity, for I am certain that all were as discomfited as I.

At first the conversation bubbled among the seven of us remaining — six, truly, for Mary remained as silent as she had through most of the afternoon. Soon, however, the group broke into small salons, as it were. Georgiana was asking Augustina and Mr. Lackey about the whole question of *fish* and *formulae*. Kitty and Thomas were also discussing fish, though I believe that may not truly have been the actual topic of interest to either of them. I was just about to join them — afraid that Kitty might yet have too much of Lydia in her — when I noted Mary gazing at Augustina. I asked her if she were serving as Mr. Shelley's secretary. She blinked at me and, without answering my query, asked *me* whether I liked the poem. I said that it was very pretty, and that I would have to read the rest to know what the total effect might be (though I did not say that I have no intention of reading any more of the poem if I can help it).

For the first time, she smiled, and while leavening so solemn a face should have seemed pleasant, yet there was something rather disturbing about the young girl's grin. It was as if she had seen my evasion for what it was and been amused by it. I was about to ask whether she had known Mr. Shelley long, when she leaned over and asked me what I thought of Augustina, whose copper locks were flying gloriously as she attempted to explain something about *steam* to Georgiana. I answered Mary, quite honestly, that I found Miss Giniver *quite interesting* and extremely intelligent, and Mary leaned even closer and whispered, "I'm apt to get tousy-mousy with ginger swots."

I have no idea what she might have meant by that, nor, in the moment, did I know how I should respond. I believe I said, "Ah," or "How nice" or something of the sort, and she once again shared her unsettling smile.

Some time later, Lady Malkin returned, looking just as well appointed as she had when she had greeted us — except that her golden hair was now bejeweled over her right ear with some pearlescent dew. A few months ago, I should not have known what to make of these droplets.

Unlearned as I may still be, I know now with certainty what they were, and what they represented. Indeed, I enjoyed very similar pearls in my hair and upon my cheek and chin the morning of your departure.

I console myself that, however pleasantly Lady Malkin and Mr. Shelley may have disported themselves in the Hermitage, they did not take in their diversions the joy that you and I did, yesterday morning in my tub.

Yesterday morning — was it truly but yesterday morning? So near and yet so far way!

Soon after, I begged our hostess's pardon and ordered the coach. As we said our goodbyes, I whispered to Lady Malkin, "You have something in your hair."

I shall probably suffer for that, but I rather enjoyed her look of wide-eyed shock.

Our ride back was somewhat less energetic than earlier in the afternoon. Kitty was asking Georgiana questions about Thomas, which your sister attempted to answer politely; I can see why young Mr. Giniver is *not for her*, and am, like you, relieved that this is so. In an attempt to distract my sister from her latest infatuation, I asked the girls what they had thought of Mr. Shelley's poem. Georgiana used that phrase again — *quite interesting* — while Kitty snorted and said she wasn't sure what it was about, but la! It was very pretty.

Which got us all talking for a bit, and while our sisters enjoyed the reading rather more than I did, I gather that our opinion of the piece was of a mind.

I meant to ask them what they had been reading yesterday that caused them so much consternation. However, we soon arrived back at beautiful Pemberley. And Mrs. Reynolds had several domestic matters that required my attention — though if she or I were being honest, she simply required that I confirm what she had already set in motion. (A new maid is needed in the scullery, since Fanny Lewis, whom I know I have met but am ashamed that I cannot remember, is getting married and moving into town, and some linens must be replaced for the guest bedrooms. I was forced to pause and take several slow breaths before acceding to Mrs. Reynolds's recommendations, since the cost of the linens alone would send my mother into weeks of bed-ridden nerves.)

After dinner, I was wandering through the halls of our house seeking any diversion aside from dreaming of you (a diversion so constant of late that I fear that it may become my only occupation) when I heard Georgiana once again playing upon the pianoforte. I followed the sound at first out of pleasure at hearing her play — but as soon as I entered the room, I could see that Kitty once again was reading, and once again in French. No sooner had I joined them than Kitty slid the volume down beside her in the chair. Tonight, however, I did not leave them. I found a copy of George Chapman's translation of *The Odyssey*, which I had heard was wonderful, and settled in to read. I had hoped that Kitty might start reading again or that they might talk, but Georgiana simply played on, and Kitty began to work on some piece of embroidery.

I found myself reading through the opening of Homer's epic. I always forget that it starts with Telemachus and Penelope. And I found myself thinking of her, waiting for her husband — and thinking, if she can wait patiently for a score of years for her love to return, surely I can wait a fortnight or less?

I do not know that I am capable of her patience, however.

Such thoughts soon led me to wish Kitty and Georgiana a good night, and back to our chamber, where I have been spilling onto this lovely paper the tale of my day to you. It is nigh on midnight, and I have been scribbling away for lo, these many hours — oh, that you were here, and I could simply report the day's events to you! And then I could kiss you, and caress you, and release us both from the bonds of our clothing so that you might ravish me, there on our bed, as you have so often.

I have made the mistake of reading your letters again — especially this morning's. How is it that splashes of ink on a piece of paper can render in me such a state of readiness for your physical presence? And yet it is so. I have lain in our big bed, stroking myself as you have stroked me and stoked me to ecstasy. My own touches were but ghosts of yours, however they have rendered me sufficiently jelly-like that I must go to sleep. I had meant to send this, but now my greatest hope is that Florry will once again deliver word from you as I wake. In the meantime, I shall dream of you.

~~I love your~~ [SCRATCHED OUT]

It is morning, and Florry did indeed burst in with a letter from you (whom I did dream of, and while the dream has dissipated like April snow, I know that it was a very, very pleasant one), once again delivered by the post boy with urgent admonition that the missive be delivered immediately to no hand but that of the lady of the house.

I am certain that we have now inspired tittering gossip not only throughout our household, but across the whole of the Midlands. Yet as before, I find that I can feel no shame: let all of England know how I love you, and let them know that I am yours.

I am sorry that your journey was delayed, yet delighted that the delay meant that your latest letter arrived so soon. I know that you had hoped to arrive in London by midday today. I hope that you shall not be there too late tonight.

I shall direct Grouse to load the gun for wolf and fire at will. I am certain that the emerald gown shall make an excellent trophy in the sitting room — next to the buck's head, perhaps. I shall also ask him to introduce me to all of the creatures and trees by name. If I am to be lady of Pemberley, I should know all of my neighbors.

It seems that my husband, my dearest Darcy, dreams of my *tongue and lips* upon his *cock?* Of placing his *Upstanding Member for Cockshire* into my *Parliamentary Organ?* His *Instrument of Delight* over my *Velvet Quail Pipe?* His *Red-headed Champion* within my *Cave of Wonders?* Well, that's probably another act altogether, but I assure you, I too dream of such things, and embrace myself in so dreaming.

Poor Harrison. If only I were there with you, I could have cleaned up your *mess* with my *extraordinary organs*. Alas!

Please assure yourself, my beloved, that your writing of your thoughts of me communicated anything but *unease*, unless it be of the most wonderful possible sort. Reading them in our bed, with the bedclothes pulled down and my linen shift pulled up, with one hand clutching your letter and the other teasing at my *Cave of Wonders,* your description of your delight gave me pleasure that I cannot even begin to describe — though to return your gift I shall attempt to do so.

The dream to which I helped myself finally find relief last night was of you, lying gloriously naked in our bed. Forgive me for saying so, love, since I know you do not like to hear it, but your beauty literally takes my breath from me. In my mind, your hand is upon your cock (your *manhood*, your *staff of love,* et cetaera), slowly burgeoning beneath your fingers, yet your eyes are upon me, as I slowly let the silk chemise I know you love fall to my feet, leaving me, like you, completely unclothed.

I must here admit to you something that I have only rarely admitted even to myself — I do not believe myself to be lovely. Truly — I am not being falsely modest nor hoping that you will gainsay me — compared to most of the women in my family, I have always felt that I was quite homely: nose too large, face too narrow, breasts uneven, scrawny of arm and leg. Yet you make me feel like the most beautiful of women, and it is that feeling — of your eyes gazing upon my naked form and seeing something wonderful there — that makes my pulse race and the juices within me *flow.*

In my waking dream last night, as I crossed the floor toward you, your dark eyes full of fire following me, I knew what we were about to do — to *fuck,* and to *fuck* long and hard. And yet it was not dreaming of the act itself that brought me to blessed release (to *pop my cork,* as Hill would have so delicately put it). It was the imagined (and remembered) sight of you — beautiful, virtuous, self-contained you — enraptured by me, by the anticipation of my approach that brought me to bliss.

Ah, me, Darcy. Like you, I have made a mess. I have made wet both my fingers and the linens beneath my cunt (*fanny, cleft of delight,* et cetaera). Think of that as you read. Do you touch yourself? I hope that you do.

You have made the whole of my body *sing* — with just the thought of you. How might it *scream* were you here indeed?

I must dress, or I shall laze in bed all day, and what would Mrs. Reynolds think of me?

Florry has helped to prepare me for the day in the green linen gown that you love so — she is much subdued, however. I wonder why?

Your warning about Georgiana's admiration for the poetry of Mr. Shelley & Co would have served your silly wife excellently had she not already done as she always does and opened her mouth to share her opinion before thinking. Whatever shall you do with me, Darcy? Your aunt's scathing judgment of me, that I am an *unfeeling, selfish girl,* is fresh in my ear now. I am fortunate that your sister (my new sister) is more thoughtful and considerate than I, for she seems to have forgiven me the lack of taste in matters literary that she believes me to have displayed. Also, I surmise that she was considerably less impressed by Shelley the man than she had been by his poems. My father is fond of saying that he prefers to enjoy his own company in his library, since to venture forth and meet one's heroes is to be disappointed. While I think that my father would prefer to stay in his library no matter whom he might encounter, Georgiana may have learned the truth of his *bon mots*.

If she or Kitty ask me about yesterday's sudden departure of our hostess and the poet, I am not sure how I should answer them. I am trying to think whether I object to their behaviour out of prudishness? Out of a prejudice against both the lady and the gentleman — though I have of late learned the dangers of prejudice so clearly?

As I write those lines, it occurs to me that my anger is due at least in part to the disregard the pair of them showed — to her guests, to her children, to Lord Malkin. To odd Mary, whatever her relationship to Mr. Shelley may be. That they indulge in pleasures similar in kind if not in meaning to those we have shared, I do not think that I feel fit to judge. That they show so little consideration for the feelings of others, that I cannot forgive.

You, however, I can always forgive, Darcy, and forgive again. Yet I cannot help but wonder — what is there to forgive? You were an inexperienced boy. She was and is a beautiful woman. Dislike her as I do, I cannot deny her *arts and allurements,* as beloved Aunt Catherine would say. Do not punish yourself further, my love. Leave that task to your wife.

I find it amusing that both of us were thinking of Ulysses and Penelope yesterday. I dearly hope, however, that it is not an omen. I truly do not think that I should survive a twenty-year's absence from your light.

I shall send this, hoping that it will find you safely in London.

Irretrievably, inconsolably, irrevocably yours,

Elizabeth Anne Bennet Darcy

PS As you can tell, I too would dearly love to watch *you* embrace yourself.
EABD

PPS Whether you are my bondsman or not, I am your slave. Let us be kind masters each to the other, then — except when it might entertain us both to be a tad cruel. EABD

PPS On the subject of euphemisms for bodily parts, the local youth of Meryton were wont to call the female pudenda (*cunt, vagina,* et cetaera) her *kitty.* As I am sure that you can appreciate, my youngest sister but one was mightily offended by this. At her insistence, the whole of my family (well, the girls and servants, at least) refer to a woman's *tunnel of delight, cleft of bliss,* et cetaera, as her *pussy.* I prefer *cunt,* however. *Virile prosody,* et cetaera. EABD

PPPS You dream of all of your *favourite* parts of me when you seek relief? I am most intrigued, husband, to discover just which parts of me those might be. EABD

PPPPS I must delay no further. I must post this while it is still morning if it is to reach you any time soon. Mrs. Reynolds says that it takes at least *two days* for a letter to reach the capital. The idea of waiting four days or more for your reply is beyond what I can bear. Yet bear it I must, as your Penelope. And the sooner this leaves to reach the post-coach, the sooner it will reach you.

PPPPPS My cunt (*pussy, kitty, mount pleasant, garden of delight,* et cetaera) weeps for you yet. Do not subject me to too long a drought of your presence, please, Darcy. I seal this with a kiss of such tempestuous passion as should blow this letter to Berkeley Square. And hopefully bring your reply back. EABD

6 – Not a War

From Fitzwilliam Darcy to Elizabeth Darcy

Nr 12, Berkeley Sqr
London
August 17

My Dearest Mrs. Darcy,

I arrived in London after the sun had set. I had tried to start this letter while still on the road from Northampton. However, the quality of the roads after this wet summer, combined with Starkey, the driver, following my admonition to make all haste, made writing *en route* impossible. (While none are broken, I cannot be certain that none of my bones have been dislocated from each other. How I wish you were here to minister to me!) And so I was reduced to thinking of what I *might* write to you. I find, as I write these lines, that planning a letter for some twelve hours does not in fact make it any easier to write, and that, perhaps, the opposite may be true.

I had held a secret hope that there would be a letter from you at our London home to brighten my arrival — a vain hope, and a silly one, since how could the post have outrun our coachman, determined, as he was, to arrive in good time? Nevertheless, the housekeeper, Mrs. Martin, was well prepared for my arrival. Harrison, Starkey, and I were all treated to a hot meal, and the servants drew me a steaming bath. This bath soothed my aches much, though your presence would have soothed them far more.

Too, it brought me in mind of our farewell, but two days ago. (Fifty-seven hours. And twenty-eight minutes.)

I think that, once I return to Pemberley, we shall spend our hours either in the bath or in the bed.

I am looking now at the large bed that Mrs. Martin installed in our room. *Our* bed in *our* house, and yet you have never seen it, and I shall rest in it, once again, alone.

Perhaps, since I am sleeping in our bed (in Berkeley Square) and you are sleeping in our bed (at Pemberley), we are sleeping together. Whether this is sophistry or mysticism (neither a turn of mind that I can abide), I wish it to be true.

In your second letter, you engaged in a brief fancy, imagining yourself as you are now being the lady who initiated me (as I was at fifteen) into the mysteries of adult intimacy — *fucking* not least but not sole among them. Oh, Elizabeth, how I wish that it had been you who had taught me what it meant to be a man. My tutor, the mistress of Langley Park, taught me, through her actions and through her words, that to be a man with respect to women was to wage a war for supremacy — and that first and foremost, in order to maintain the upper hand, one must defend the bastion of one's privacy. She did not *steal* my virginity — that I was willing enough at the time to give her, flattered as I was by the attentions of a golden-haired, worldly, pretty older woman. Yet she robbed me of my innocence, by giving me so sad and so cynical an experience of relations between the sexes. It was a lesson that I scarcely knew that I had learned — until you taught me its fallacy over the past weeks and months.

It is only part of my shame to have taken that lesson to heart, but it is a part I could well wish I had never heard, nor embraced.

I know that, were you to have welcomed young Fitzwilliam Darcy (son and heir) to your bed, he should have been the most blest of boys — and indeed of men. Blest by your beauty. Blest by your generosity of spirit and by the ferocity of your compassion. Blest by your enduring patience as well as by your overflowing passion. What you might have got out of the bargain I cannot even begin to imagine — yet *he* should have learned lessons that *I* am only now beginning to struggle with — that the love of man and woman is not a *war*, but a journey of exploration, a *game* in which the only way to *win* was to win together. That giving pleasure (of all kinds) can be as rewarding as receiving it. They are precepts that I look forward to your continuing to teach me for many, many years.

But first, I wish with all my heart to see you again — to hold you and to taste you, every part of you — to taste the nectar that moistens your lips above and below. To taste the heat of your rising passion as I ride you — or as you ride me. A part of Lady Malkin's errant tutelage was the supposed truism that to be on top was to *win*. The fallacy of that conclusion is blindingly apparent to me now. Were you here, in all of your glory, atop me now, I should consider myself the most complete of *winners*.

Ah. You have inspired yet another ecstasy in me — imagining your gracious, pale form above me, around me. You have, indeed, greatly soothed my body from the aches of the long journey — though I know that your presence could do far more to make me feel better.

This time, I came prepared. A handkerchief caught what my body intended to deposit *within you*, and so Harrison shall not have to see nor see *to* stains upon my trousers. I am sure that he is as relieved as I in this.

Relieved as I am of some of the agitation engendered by your absence, I know that I must to our lonely bed soon — yet I must ask a question about one passage in your letter to me. You mentioned playing as a young girl a game called *Tom-o'-Straw*. What sort of game was this?

Whatever it may have been, I know that I should have loved to play it with the young Lizzy (hellion) — scabby knees and all.

Tomorrow morning, my factor Kite arrives just past breakfast to discuss a number of matters of some urgency. Mr. Gardiner is due too in the afternoon. The day will be a full and productive one, I hope, and yet I cannot stop myself from wishing that I could simply order one of the horses saddled and ride post-haste back to Pemberley and your side.

With faith, with hope, with love,
Yours,

Fitzwilliam Henry, Darcy by birth
(Bennet by God's good Grace)

PS I do hope that you will discover whom our sisters are reading. While as I said, in general the worst of the volumes in the library are at most titillating (if not a bit silly), there is at least one author whose works I should not wish *anyone* to stumble across without due preparation if at all, and whom I cannot imagine either of our sisters having the education to appreciate for those limited literary virtues possessed by his books. — FHD(B)

PPS Do not ever apologise for wishing to say that you miss or desire me. I miss and desire you with all of my body and soul. That you are suffering the same distress makes me feel, if no better, at least less alone in feeling ill. Perhaps this is a defect in my character, but I feel that I can bear anything — if I can bear it with you. — FHD(B)

PPS When you *bear* in fact, we shall do that too together. — FHD(B)

PPPS I do hope that Lady Malkin was not too dreadful in her attentions during your visit. Again, I do not believe the lady to be *evil*, yet I know her to be ungracious of spirit, however graceful she may be in form. I am certain that she sees you as a competitor, and, as I noted above, I know that she always likes to *win*. — FHD(B)

PPPS I shall send Harrison out with this to seek a rider headed north. It is yet early enough that — if we are fortunate — this may yet reach you by late post tomorrow or, more likely, the morning post on Wednesday. I know that you (with your sense of thrift and of propriety) are likely to berate me for even considering the expense, but it seems only prudent to hire an express courier to bear our letters the hundred and fifty-seven miles from here to Pemberley and back. To have gone a whole day without a letter from you is unutterable agony. — FHD(B)

PPPPS It is a greater joy than I can tell you to have *the full measure of my delight* overflow within you — and out of you. Kissing that overflow from your lips (above and below) has become a delight that I treasure more than I could ever have imagined. — FHD(B)

7 – Some Tiresome Epistolary Romance

From Elizabeth Darcy to Fitzwilliam Darcy

Pemberley, Derbyshire, *August 18/19*

My dearest Darcy,

There was no letter from you this morning — and while I had hoped for none, I was nonetheless set adrift when Florry solemnly entered our room, no missive in hand, and opened the drapes. I remained adrift as I bathed (without you to scrub my back), dressed, and broke my fast. At a loss for what to do with myself — and promising myself that I would not simply spend the day writing you again — and since I could not find either of our sisters — I wandered the lovely halls of Pemberley, introducing myself to your dark, brooding ancestors. Your father's portrait and I had a lovely chat; we discussed his son's many virtues, as well as his unfortunate choice in wife. Your father assured me that, however multifold my shortcomings, I was unlikely to be the worst of the mistresses of Pemberley.

I went into the library, hoping for some indication as to what book has so captured interests as divergent as Kitty's and Georgiana's. Sadly, there were no stray volumes of French prose lain suspiciously about (nor of French verse, for that matter). I must speak with the staff, as they are clearly far too good at their work.

I picked up my good friend Homer once again and read on in the first book of the *Odyssey*, a tussle of wills between Penelope and her son, where he asks her not to subject herself to the riotous suitors who nightly invade their home. I found myself reading this familiar passage, for the first time, not from the perspective of the child, but of the mother. How must she feel, to have her son play the man of the house with her for the first time? Annoyed, certainly, since she has managed affairs to that point well enough (though, worthy wife of wily Odysseus as she may be, she has not managed to sweep the house clean of drunken louts). Proud, perhaps, to see her boy becoming a man. I must imagine that her feelings in this case are complex.

And I am, myself, somewhat astonished to realise that I have begun to consider myself in the mother's place, rather than the child's. It is not a place I feel prepared for — and yet is any of us ever truly prepared for life's greatest challenges and opportunities? One hopes one shall be ready — that one shall rise to the occasion with strength and compassion. When I think back upon our exchanges, first in Meryton, and then at Rosings, I know that I did not acquit myself as I might have wished, even in the moment. When I first met you, I spoke as a child, I thought as a child, and I understood as a child. But once I came truly to know you (and to *know* you), I began to put away childish things, and speak, think, and understand as a woman. And so now, as I read anew a book that I have read many times (though never in this lovely translation), I am astonished to read it with a woman's eyes.

You are kind to tell me that you might ever have thought me in *any* way perfect, since I have, as your father and I discussed at such great length, so many defects and imperfections, not least my lack of facility in tongues. My father did his best to inculcate in us some skill at French and at Latin (our mother, of course, was no help) — yet it was the one lesson that I somehow could never master. Of natural philosophy, history, and English letters I was always a most capable and willing student. Not, however, foreign tongues. Whether my lack of mastery reflects poor tuition, poor study, some defect in my own faculties, or some combination of the three, I do not know — since ignorance *cannot* know what it does not know. Therefore no, I have never enjoyed Racine, nor

Villon, nor Moliere, nor yet Seneca, Horace, Sappho, nor any other of your heathen, libertine French, Roman, and Greek poets in their native languages. Perhaps *you* could teach me? I must submit that I am most I awe of your lingual skills, and should greatly appreciate your applying those skills to my betterment. Do you think this might be a lesson that you might be willing to apply to my elevation? I should be a most, most willing pupil. And, of course, should be most desirous of demonstrating to you everything that I have learned.

I am a fool, it seems. Yet I am your fool. Do with me as you will.

Once I had finished the first book of Homer's masterwork, I found myself following my feet, which led me to, of all places, the Pemberley kitchens. At Longbourn, Mrs. Hill's domain served as the heart of our home — every member of the household could be found there at some time of day, even my father. In winter cold, it was the warmest place in the house; in summer heat, the most open to the outdoors. I suppose I had imagined that I might find our sisters there, sharing morning tea (or, in Georgiana's case, chocolate) around a table with Mrs. Reynolds and the cook, Mrs. Patchett. No such cosy scene presented itself, however. The Pemberley kitchens are, I discovered, a veritable Temple of Vesta, with all of the attendants such a place of worship might employ. (Whether those attendants might qualify as Vestals I cannot say. I assume solely from her title that Mrs. Patchett does not, and I know that the soon-to-be-nuptialed Miss Lewis shows no aspirations toward such a life.) Some dozen or so members of the staff were busily engaged in the work of keeping our large household fed — two women kneading dough at a large, flour-covered table, three more chopping a mass and variety of vegetables that would have been the entire summer production of our kitchen garden at Longbourn, two girls plucking what looked to be the carcasses of some half-dozen or so geese, while several attended the altar of the stoves under Mrs. Patchett's imperious supervision, and others flew to and from the hidden treasury of the stores, carrying mysterious supplies to and fro.

On the day of our wedding, when you introduced me to the household as your wife and the new mistress of Pemberley, I was so overcome with joy and pleasure (and anticipation of joy and pleasure soon to follow) that I do not believe that I truly took in the scale of the army that toils to maintain the beautiful house and grounds, to maintain the livestock — and to maintain and feed all of the inhabitants, including the servants themselves. Dining these past weeks with you, our sisters, and Mrs. Annesley, before she departed to visit her sister — or even on those occasions when we have been visited by Jane and Charles or by my parents — though the room was grander and the attendants at table more numerous than at Longbourn, it has been easy for me to forget how much *larger* my new home is than my old one, and how many people's labour it takes to make my own life so *free* of labour.

No sooner had I entered the enormous kitchen than the entire congregation stopped their kneading, plucking, chopping, cooking, and to-and-fro-ing. The whole kitchen was silent, but for the crackle of the fire and the bubbling of the pots.

"Mistress Darcy," said Mrs. Pratchett, wiping her hands upon her apron.

"Please do not let me disturb your work," I pleaded. Desperate to seem to have some reason for invading their sacred space, I continued, "I only wished to convey my best wishes to Miss Lewis."

The whole of the assembly smiled and nodded, and I felt a flush of pleasure at having acquitted myself passably as *Mistress Darcy*, this once at least!

The young maid (soon to be maid no longer in *any* sense) was encouraged by the rest to stand and approach me. She was one of the goose-pluckers, and tufts of down powdered her cap and shoulders. Raw-boned and wide-faced, she stood before me, her expression shy yet somehow full of hungry anticipation.

I managed to burble out what I thought was a suitably happy speech on the felicity of marriage and hoping that she and her husband to be blest with the kind of happiness that you and I have found. Truly, I felt I was most fulsome and eloquent, giddy newlywed that I myself am.

The congregants in the kitchens nodded and smiled some more, and, as I came to the end of my little epithalamium, I could sense that same hungry anticipation growing, not just from Fanny Lewis, but from the whole company.

I stood there.

They stood there.

And then I left.

I know that I was supposed to do something — that they expected something more of me than my words, however happy. Yet I could not think what it was that I was supposed to do. Having begun my first campaign into the depths of Pemberley so successfully, then, I ended in utter rout.

I should have asked Mrs. Pathcett what I ought to have done, or gone and sought out Mrs. Reynolds's advice. Yet I felt so ashamed — and so incapable of understanding my shame — that I instead retreated to our bedroom, where I have hidden, not wanting to show my face.

I feel as if I have not only failed somehow to fulfill my role as the lady of the house, but as your wife. I find myself wishing that you were here to correct my mistake, yet glad that you are gone, and so did not see it. I know that I am being silly, and yet cannot stop myself.

I did not come to dinner, but asked Florry to bring my food to our room.

Though it looked delicious, I could not eat the goose.

Perhaps I shall hide away here for the rest of my tenure at Pemberley. I shall take up weaving and become your Penelope indeed.

Kitty and Georgiana came to be sure I was not ill. I assured them I was not — they nodded and looked at each other in such a way that I was given the impression that they believe me to be pining for you.

True enough! Ah, me. I am become the heroine from some tiresome epistolary romance, wasting away, alone and unloved, sending pleading letters to the stern object of her affections.

Of course, I am speaking with them as I write this to you, so I am not quite *alone*, nor, I suppose that I must admit, am I quite *unloved*. I am in the company of our very sweet, very different sisters, trying very hard neither to scold nor to laugh at them. I am doing my best to keep all of my smirking confined to this foolscap, in any case, since I could not bear to laugh in Georgiana's face. I do not reckon the subsequent subterfuge to be her doing, in any case, though subterfuge was clearly in the offing.

When I asked how they had spent their day, they once again glanced at each other — it seems Kitty has recruited Gigi (as she calls Georgiana) into the conspiracy of the younger sisters, a plot I know of old. They both looked down at their skirts and mumbled about walking on the grounds, in the direction of Lambton and Langley Park.

When I asked if they had encountered anyone, Georgiana looked up like a startled faun, while my sister Kitty stood, eyes wide, her usually mercurial face at once statue-still. Why, yes, as it happens, they had *happened* to come upon the young Giniver siblings, who *happened* to be out riding. Oh, and that odd girl, Mary, had *happened* lurking about as well. Just by happenstance.

I hope that you shall reward me at some future point for not bursting into a storm of laughter at this farce. As [SCRATCHED OUT]

Well.

My.

The most remarkable apparition has just visited us.

As I was about to question our sisters more deeply, there came a knock upon the door. At my invitation, Florry let in a man of mud and clay — as are all men, but this one's clothes and exposed skin were a uniform earthen colour except for the insides of his legs. And in his hand there was grime-covered, sealed letter. "M-madam," the figure croaked, and, when I had taken the packet from him, collapsed in a cloud of dust upon the floor.

Georgiana and Kitty raced to care for the extraordinary visitor, yet I will not be ashamed to admit that all of my attention remained fixed on the message that he had delivered to me — from you, my lord and husband.

As I unsealed your letter with trembling fingers, Florry brought water to Georgiana who dipped her handkerchief in the basin and used it delicately to clear the begrimed man's face. Before I had a chance to read more than your now-familiar, much-beloved salutation (I hope that I shall remain not only your *dearest Mrs. Darcy* for some time yet, but your *only* Mrs. Darcy for at least a few months), the prostrate messenger coughed and stirred. With a start, he gazed up into the eyes of his ministering angel and spake in a voice of wonder (with a pronounced London accent): "Physician Nature, le' my spirit blood! Oh, ease my 'eart of verse and le' me rest!"

Georgiana met this extraordinary declaration with a blush and the dumbfounded look it deserved. Kitty, for her part, giggled, which set Florry (who has seemed subdued of late) tittering too. Together, the three graces stood the young man up. Moved less, I must confess, by compassion than by a desire to read your words in private, I suggested that they lead him to the kitchens to see him fed, and to ask Mrs. Reynolds to find him a bed.

"Bu' madam," the bedraggled courier demurred, "I'm supposed to bring back your answer to Mr. Darcy."

"And you shall have it," I said, "but not until the morning. Have you ridden all the way from London?"

"Ay. Since last night."

"Did you not sleep, sir?" Georgiana asked, seeming most concerned.

He gave a shrug and nodded. "In the stable at Northampton, where I changed horses. Miss."

"Well, then, sir," I said, "you shall sleep in a better bed tonight. Go with these ladies and see what our cook can find you to eat, and Florry, see if perhaps a bath may be found to wash the road from him and to soothe his bones, for he has done us a great service."

Florry curtsied, and the young messenger gave an awkward attempt at a bow, then followed the girls out of my room, a cloud of dust in his wake.

And then I fell upon your letter like a she-wolf upon a deer after a long winter's fast.

Oh, my dearest, dearest Darcy! Your letter made me feel — to leap to a different metaphor altogether — like a prisoner who has been locked in darkness for years but is suddenly released into the sun. Yes, I am aware that I received your last letter only yesterday morning, yet I had begun to steel myself to the possibility that another message from you might not reach me for days yet. And so, while as you say my maternally inculcated sense of thrift is scandalised by your hiring a private courier for a purpose of no greater import than to carry your words to me and mine to you, yet I am deeply touched that you have chosen to do so, and am delighted that you have chosen to allow me to (if I may jump into a yet another entirely different realm of metaphor) bathe in your words, and so in your imagined presence. That your messenger was a Cockney with the apparent soul of a poet seems all the more wonderful. (His silhouette is still marked in dust upon the floor. I find it a pleasing decoration, if only because it assures me that I did not imagine his arrival, nor your love.)

I have made the mistake of reading your letter through without disrobing. Silly Elizabeth, you should have known that, sooner or later, your husband's text would send your hands and fingers searching beneath your gown's hem and over its bodice to tease with flesh those parts that his letter excited with words. I am seated at the lovely writing desk beside our bed — facing away from the door — and while I started reading dressed as decorously as a lady of the manor should be, I see that my skirts are now above my hips and the lace meant to cover my collarbone below my breasts. How could reading how I had *relieved the agitation engendered by my absence* not spark that agitation in me? How could I not read of your imagining me atop you without myself imagining you *within me*? How could I read such orgasms of prose committed to *tasting every part of me* and not be moved to orgasms of passion myself? And so I was, dearest Darcy, by my own touch in part, but by your words most of all.

Ah, to feel you within me now — to feel that *overflow* we both so love, spilling out of me. To feel your *extraordinary organs* cleaning the overflow from my thighs, from my *cunt*.

Even thinking of it has brought me to another ecstasy, husband, and I must reward you for so moving me to pleasure. I shall continue to attempt to convey your reward in this letter, but be certain, Fitzwilliam Henry, that your reward upon your return shall be protracted and most thorough, and shall be repeated at length and in depth.

Still you talk of shame regarding Lady Malkin. Abandon shame, my love, since she has long since done so. Any lessons she may have thought to teach you, you have learned better and more recently — I should like to be able to claim that I was your tutor in any way, but we both know that the lesson of True Love is one that you took to heart before you knew me (or *knew* me), else would you have married Caroline Bingley without a second thought. Any penance that you might have felt deserved from the actions of young Fitzwilliam Darcy (son and heir) has long since been served — although I might argue that you deserved none. Were an army of Countess Malkins to have seduced you — ay, and their maids as well! — your present propriety and delicacy are so beyond impeachability that anyone who knows you would join me to beg you doff your vestments of sack and hair and go —

Well, your wife would wish you always to go as God created you.

I cannot imagine a more fitting costume for so beautiful and so noble man than no costume at all. Yet I know that neither your sister nor mine would welcome your going about the house in such a state, nor am I willing to share that glory with anyone. Your bum in particular is a piece of Nature's art too exquisite for any eyes but mine to behold, and so I must ask you to go clothed after all.

Ah, another small ecstasy, and all inspired by the thought of kissing your cheeks — the nether ones.

I must array myself once more, or — facing away from the door or not — I shall seem so debauched were anyone to enter that they should have a very clear idea of what I have been doing for this past hour, and what parts of me I would wish you yourself to be addressing. I am not yet so lost a creature that I cannot stop playing with myself. I can stop — indeed I can — though I must confess that I do not *wish* to do so.

I must confess too that I was moved beyond words by your postscript, saying that if — nay, *when* — I bear, we shall bear together. I wish nothing more than to carry your children, knowing the offspring of so marvelous a sire must be miraculous indeed.

Yet since you know already how far I am from perfect, so must I reveal to you that, like most women, I fear childbirth. One thing to fear of course is my own mortality — as you and your sister must I am sure understand. Yet too there is another fear, engendered by attending upon my own mother through two stillbirths, of losing that which I have not yet had.

And so knowing that, when I am faced with the possibility of either joy or tragedy, I shall not face it alone — that quells my heart and touches my soul in ways that I know I cannot even begin to express, even Lizzy Bennet, who never found herself tongue-tied in any company! I can no other answer give but thanks.

Your parlays with Uncle Edward and with the estimable Mr. Kite should, I believe, be done. I hope that your business was as prosperous as it always seems to be. Should you see Aunt or Uncle Gardiner again, please convey my love and best wishes.

You ask me what kind of a game *Tom o' Straw* might be and I was at first astonished that you did not know it — it was a very popular game among the children in our corner of Hertfordshire. Young Lizzy Bennet (hellion) played at it incessantly, both with her sisters, with Charlotte and Maria Lucas, and with the boys and girls who lived near us. And yet when I tried just now to recall and describe the game, I have found myself reverting to spoiling lovely linens sheets once more, and not the sort of spoiling, nor the sorts of linen sheets, for which both of us long.

It was a very complicated game, that much I remember, and it centered around a scarecrow. It involved much running, and more than a little wrestling, so that my mother was always berating us for being unladylike, while Mrs. Hill was always berating us for dirtying our clothes.

Beyond that I cannot remember the details much, though I should very much like to. Perhaps you and I could find a straw man in the fields here in Derbyshire and play ourselves? Do you think Mrs. Reynolds would be much dismayed at us if we were to come back bestained and besmirched? Or would she simply be amused at two adults playing at being children together?

That hellion Lizzy would have dearly loved to play with so serious and so handsome a boy as you. And so would this hellion, Elizabeth.

It is now morning. I shall seek out our Cupid and send him flying south with this letter. May it find you happy and bring you still greater happiness.

Without fear, without restraint, without breath, yours,

Elizabeth Anne Bennet Darcy

PS Try though she might, Lady Malkin has not nor never shall win — not with you, and not with your wife. And whichever of us may happen to be *on top*, you and I both know that when we are joined in body as we are in soul, we shall both of us *always* be victorious. EABD

PPS Now you have told me of this scandalous author upon whose works you *would not wish for anyone to stumble across without due preparation*, I become fascinated to find out who this paragon of vice might be! Is his work (I believe you said it was a he?) so poor? Or is his subject so shocking? Clearly I must begin my search of Pemberley's upper shelves for myself! EABD

PPPS Husband, you have not yet told me what are your *favourite* parts of me. Is it my *cunt,* perhaps? Or yet my *breasts?* Or my *arse,* which is, I will aver (though I cannot view it directly), by no means the masterpiece that yours demonstrably is. Or those *extraordinary organs* that you remarked upon so favourably, my tongue and lips? Please, husband — your curious wife wishes to know, so that she may deliver any and all to you. EABD

8 – The Little Death

From Fitzwilliam Darcy to Elizabeth Darcy

Nr 12, Berkeley Sqr
London
August 20

My Dearest Mrs. Darcy,

Your uncle Gardiner (our uncle Gardiner?) dined with me here this evening. We had had further business to conduct, which was concluded satisfactorily on both sides, and I insisted that he stay. He asks me to extend his love and affection, and to tell you that, when you can, please to write his wife, your aunt. He tells me that the children are all yet full of excitement about our wedding, and wish to hear how you are — and Mrs. Gardiner wishes to hear her own news, which Mr. Gardiner and I agreed without saying was most likely news that neither his children nor he should wish to hear.

Your letter of the 17th did in fact find me with the evening post — exactly like a very loyal spaniel bringing the welcome prey of your words. I am dismayed to find that, as much as I thought I understood how difficult this short separation would be, I had underestimated its severity and my own need. Yet too I find that your letters are an oil to still the troubled waters of my soul.

I find that I am of more than two minds with regards to your question about Kitty calling my sister "Gigi." In the first instance, I think that Georgiana has had too few friends of her own age and sex, Augustina being the only close one I can think of, and none close enough for pet names. And so I am delighted that Catherine feels attached enough to Georgiana to re-christen her, however they name each other. At the same time, I cannot help but think of my father, who, as stern as you may ever have found me, was ever more a stickler for propriety. He was always most insistent that Georgiana and I use the proper names of things — that respect for the name increases respect for the thing, however much Herr Kant might have disagreed with that thought. And yet again, I cannot but help but think of the fact that our mother never had the opportunity to give Georgiana any name at all — and that in my memories of her, she expressed endearment fulsomely and frequently, and so perhaps she would greatly approve of your sister addressing my sister so.

For myself, I can only say that I am grateful that your sister has extended this small sign of affection to mine, and if Georgiana receives the name with pleasure, then let them call each other what they will.

Though perhaps they should eschew any pet names in Hertfordshire, since I am given to know that "Kitty" may mean something somewhat indecent among the folk thereabout.

I am sorry that you and our sisters should have had to endure such appalling behaviour from Lady Malkin and the erstwhile gentleman, Mr. Shelley. I have said that I do not believe the lady to be vicious, yet, as she proved herself to you, I cannot term her anything but venal. As you say, I cannot judge her for enjoying the pleasures of *fucking* (carnal embrace, physical congress, &c), nor, I should like to think, do I waste my passions on *hating* anyone. Yet must I admit that my *dislike* and *disaffection* toward the countess are as intractable as any that I have felt.

In some ways, it was my aversion to Elizabeth Giniver, Countess Malkin, that taught me that my feelings toward Elizabeth Bennet, now Mistress of Pemberley, were far more complex than my initial, superficial impressions might have suggested to me. Your sharpness — of vision and of tongue — may have stung my pride, that first night at the Assemblies in Meryton. Yet the clarity of that vision and the facility of that tongue (which I had would not truly come to appreciate until our wedding night), as well as all of your excellent parts (on whose excellencies I shall extol fully later), taught me to understand that, stung though I may have been, what I was feeling toward you was nothing like what I feel or felt toward Lady Malkin, but rather deep and sincere admiration and, ultimately, love. And so I suppose that, in spite of any animosity that I might feel toward her, this is yet another thing for which I must thank the lady.

The girl Mary does sound *quite interesting*. Is she of Georgiana's age, or Kitty's?

The *ginger swot* Augustina is indeed not only *quite,* but perhaps you would grant *most* interesting. Is not she a remarkable girl?

I am forced here to admit that my sister's *ardency* toward the poetry of Mr. Shelley has always somewhat bewildered me. I must admit, as well, that very little of the English poetry of the past century seems at all admirable to me. I have read Georgiana's favourites, Mr. Shelley and the hopefully less execrable Lord Byron, with little pleasure. So too have I found in Mssrs. Pope and Dryden, but also in your esteemed Mssrs. Coleridge and Blake little to admire. (Indeed, I found that Mr. Blake's art and poetry go far beyond *quite interesting* in my book, settling solidly in the chapter titled *Extremely Peculiar.*) The last English poet whose work I can say that I truly admire is the audacious Dean Donne, whose *prosody* is *virility* itself. I wish that I could say that it was his metaphysical poems that I found the most moving. However, it his love poems that I have always most *ardently* admired. Perhaps we may read some of them together when I return?

You ask what my favourite parts of you might be, but have I not already told you so? I know that Miss Bingley and I discussed them at length — I seem to remember me that it was in your presence, during your visit to Netherfield. Have you so soon forgot?

And here I must assure you of two things: first, that I admire *all* of you, unadulteratedly, without prejudice, and without compunction; and next, that if I were forced to chuse those parts of you that I prize above all others — a choice I should rather die than make — that the parts that I should then enumerate should be unseen and impalpable.

All of which is to say that, without any doubt, I certainly admire your *cunt* (mount pleasant, cleft of flesh, cave of wonders, fanny, &c) and too your *breasts* (*mounts* pleasant, diddies, buttery bar, twin peaks, &c).

All the more, I am astonished (which is not to say a trifle shocked) to find that a gentlewoman of such refined and accomplished tastes as my wife should be a connoisseur of that least refined and most accomplished in (admittedly occasionally delightful) vulgarity of English novels, *Memoirs of a Woman of Pleasure*. I feel that perhaps we should discuss this too when I return? Also, do I need to tell your father to install taller book-shelves at Longbourn?

It might now be appropriate for your husband to aver that, indeed, he dreams of placing his Upstanding Member in your *most extraordinary* Parliamentary Organ. Indeed, he dreams of doing so. He dreams too of applying his Clapper (Red Rag, tongue, &c) to her Venerable Monosyllable (*pudendum muliebre,* quim, Pleasure Conduit, cunt, &c) to bring her to Bliss (Let-Go, the Little Death, &c) over and over.

Are you aware that your voice, so pleasingly low, becomes high and airy when you are in the grips of said Little Death? That sound (and the pleasure it signals) fills me with a greater feeling of accomplishment than any other act I have ever taken in my life — as too the sight of your body trembling and flush with rapture (Bliss, &c), or the feel of your Cave of Wonders (kitty, &c, &c) in spasms against my mouth or around my cock (Battering Ram, Staff of Love, &c, &c, &c) as I Plough your Furrow (Take Possession of Your Lady Jewel, fuck your quim, &c, &c, &c, &c). I love that sound. I love it dearly. I miss it.

It seems that I miss it so that I have made more work for poor Harrison. In struggling to undo my flies and unleash my &c, &c, &c, I was brought to my own Little Death. I have exploded at the mere *thought* of your pleasure, of pleasuring you, as if I were the boy Fitzwilliam Darcy (son and heir) once more. Do not be so sure that you would enjoy teaching such an excitable creature as I was then — for he (or rather I) should give out at the mere thought or barest sight of you in all your glory, and he (or rather I) should never engage you in any form of carnal intercourse (intimate embrace, sexual congress, &c) before you had quite overcome me.

And here I must assure you of something that you apparently do not believe: not only are you lovely — and lovely in every imaginable manner — but as I told you when I came to you in your bath, your raw and incandescent beauty is beyond my capacity to observe let alone to express. You are the thing-itself of beauty. Beauty is you. You are beautiful beyond the tongue of man to describe or the eye of man to paint. Do not speak to me of scrawny legs or arms, and I certainly refuse to hear a word spoken against your breasts. Your nose is perfect. Your body is perfect. Your eyes are transcendent. You are and shall always be the model of earthly perfection for me. Let Shakespeare sing of his dark lady and Catullus of his Lesbia, and I have already sworn to forget Mr. Alighieri's Beatrice — none shall ever surpass my Elizabeth.

I am pleased to hear that you prefer to name your pudenda your *cunt*. I want to *fuck* your *cunt* with my *cock*.

Ah, Elizabeth, my body screams for you. I hunger for you. How could I ever ride away from you?

No sooner had I begun to ask that question — no sooner had I begun to struggle to avoid making more work for my valet — then an apparition familiar to you gave a knock upon the door. I was just finishing refastening my flies when a figure all of mud strode into this room — *our* room — and knelt before me, like some battlefield messenger of old. He held out a letter — *your* letter — and said, "From your lady's hand, Mr. Darcy, sir."

I gave him a crown and sent him off with Mrs. Martin for a meal, with the promise that I would have a letter — *this* letter — for him in the morning. Once he was gone, I fell upon your letter, the second I have received today, and discovered, among many other wonderful things, that our "Cupid" made an even more dramatic entrance at Pemberley than at Berkeley Square. Nonetheless, I am predisposed to like the man, since he has brought your words to me, and with the spirit of a poet as well as a courier, it seems. Better that Georgiana be taken with a poet-messenger, I suppose, than a poet-blackguard such as Mr. Shelley.

Well, well, we have indeed both been thinking on the trials of brave Ulysses and his wife. Survive we shall, and no — there is no monster, no demigod, no Ocean shall keep me from you beyond the end of this month. Napoleon himself could cut across the middle of our island with his army and I should still return to you. Though the end of August may feel a twenty-years removed thing, yet shall we see these last, interminable days through, that I swear.

You tell me to give up shame, since Lady Malkin has none, which is true. I know that guilt and shame, like pride and prejudice, are habits of mind that, once they have imparted their lesson, can tend to weaken rather than strengthen the spirit, and so I shall attempt to do as you ask. Yet, there is so much of what transpired between myself and her — consequences that cannot simply be forgot or shrugged off — and so I am afraid that it may be the work of more than a mere moment for me to find the equanimity you suggest.

As for presenting myself to you as God made me — well, My Dearest Mrs. Darcy, I am happy to present myself so whenever you deem it proper. All of me I have promised before the Rev. Mr. Whitley and our assembled friends and family to be yours. Then you may have all of me whenever it pleases you to ask.

I must take at your word, however, the artistic merits of my *arse*. I have, I must grant, never seen it. If it give you pleasure to look upon, you may do that too, at any time. As for *kissing* it, I shall grant that if it give you pleasure to do so, I must grant that it shall give me pleasure to have it done. I know from our games together that you enjoy the feel of my lips upon your *bum*.

On the subject of games — I should love to hear more of this *Tom o' Straw*. Perhaps Mrs. Collins or one of your sisters remembers more of the game? Mrs. Reynolds must forgive us — we have a vast estate to play upon, and have scarcely yet made sufficient use of the small acreage belonging to our bed — and the bath, of course. At least if we play this game, it strikes me as likely that we shall play the whole of it clothed; then what objection can our estimable housekeeper have to our disporting ourselves? Let it not be said that we Darcys lack a joy in sport. Dignified we may strive to be, but we are no Puritans.

I am so terribly sorry that you felt that you had in any way failed to uphold your duty or mine in your foray into the redoubt of the redoubtable Mrs. Patchett. It was natural of you to visit the kitchens, and kind of you, even upon the spur of the moment, to wish Miss Lewis well on her up-coming wedding. It has been a tradition, upon a longtime servant of our household leaving our service, whether it be to be married or for any other honourable reason, that my father and now I have bestowed a gold crown and some provisions, usually something appropriate to the new life upon which they were embarking. That is most likely what Miss

Lewis and her fellows were expecting you to give her, but there was no way for you to know that. You have been a member of the household for a matter of weeks. How could you know of such an custom on our part or expectation on theirs?

I believe that Miss Lewis (who has worked in our kitchens since she was a girl) is marrying Francis Lennon, the eldest son of the innkeeper at Lambton, who was your host last summer. Perhaps if you were to tell those estimable ladies, Mrs. Reynolds and Mrs. Patchett, that you have consulted with me, and that we — *we* — should like to provide as our wedding gift to the young couple the customary gold coin, along with, perhaps, a side of beef from our stores, which will be much appreciated both by the couple and by the denizens of the Spotted Lamb. Between them, our estimable cook and housekeeper will, I am sure, be happy to help make all right.

I am all astonishment, I must admit, to find that there is any subject at which you are not only less than facile, but any less than mistress. That such a subject might be *tongues* — that strikes me as beyond astonishing. Ah, *agapimeni mou, mon amour, amata mea, meine liebeling, ladodi* — it would give me the greatest delight to apply my lingual skills for your elevation. I should be happy to apply them whenever and wherever you like — as I believe that I have stated several times above.

I shall finish this letter tonight to send off with our Cupid, should he be sufficiently recovered in the morning. Ridden to Derbyshire and back in less than seventy-two hours? I cannot believe the man is still standing! (I will here admit that, at Starkey's suggestion, we left a relay of horses between here and Pemberley against the possibility of needing just such a swift courier for our love. Our notoriety may then have stretched beyond the Midlands to the whole of England. Would you have it an other way? I would not.)

Know, however, that as I go to sleep, I shall be thinking of my *tongue* upon your *cunt*. There shall be no euphemisms in my waking dream, nor any other artifice of modesty. Only your flesh and mine.

With my heart, with my mind, with my soul,

Yours,

Fitzwilliam Henry, Darcy by birth

(Bennet by God's good Grace)

PS No, I will not speak more of the scandalous author I *hope* our sisters have not encountered — except to say that his books are *in French*, involve acts so patently unnatural that it is often difficult to see the intended delight in their description, and that it would make the most libertine of readers blush like an untutored fifteen-year-old son and heir. I do not think that Georgiana nor yet Kitty could possibly be reading such a work. Yet there are others. Please do continue your researches! — FHD(B)

PPS I hope that you do not question my favourite parts of you still. Though I would say once more that I like them *all,* suffice it to say, you are using them now. — FHD(B)

PPPS I can of a certainty state that I should never have married Caroline Bingley. I love her brother as my own, she is very pretty (though by no means so beautiful as you), and she has a sharpness of wit nearly to match yours (though not the sharpness of vision nor the warmth of heart) — yet I cannot say that I like the woman. I am humbled to admit that I could never find a way to make her understand that she was not for me without giving what seemed undue and unpardonable offense — at least, until I met you. No more would I have ever married my cousin Anne, despite her mother's protestations. I hold a strong affection for my cousin, yet I cannot imagine pledging my life to a person whose chief accomplishments seem to be staying out of a sick bed more days than not and avoiding her mother's considerable wrath. I will tell you honestly: I had hoped that my sunny friend Charles Bingley might prove the perfect champion for my mother's namesake — he is carefree as she is careworn, full of spirit as she is dispirited, and hopeful where her hopes and dreams seem to be largely unattended. Alas, she could rarely seem to rise from her sick bed when he came to Rosings, and he never seemed to show any particular affection for her — certainly not of the sort that flowered into his love for your sister Jane. All of which is to say, though there have been other women in my life, I was never meant for any but Lizzy Bennet. — FHD(B)

PPPPS I have left a trace of my passion upon this paper. You move me. — FHD(B)

[Discolouration]

PPPPPS Our Cupid, I discover, goes by the sobriquet of *Junkets*. A sweetmeat perhaps? A secret feast? He certainly provides *us* with a secret feast, you and I. In any case, I live for him to bring your reply. — FHD(B)

9 — *The Order of the Goose*

From Elizabeth Darcy to Fitzwilliam Darcy

Pemberley, Derbyshire, *August 20/21*

My dearest Darcy,

Yesterday morning brought no mudstained Cupid to our door, but two letters did arrive by the morning post and took up much of my day.

The first was from Jane. She told me that she and Charles are to see you in London. Alas! That my sister and her husband may go where they wish, and see whom they please, yet I must stay a widow in all but weeds here in Derbyshire. Why may not I too come to London? Why may I not fly to your arms and to *our bed,* there in Berkeley Square? While you are gone, the beauties of Pemberley seem flat, dull, and without savour, as if the colour had gone out of the world.

Did you observe the solar eclipse some years ago? My father, who had been reading a great deal of astronomy, had Hill fashion squares of glass smutted with soot so that we might watch the sun directly as it was engulfed in shadow. We were excited — myself and Mary most of all — and while the event was both fascinating and singular, and while our father read to us descriptions of eclipses past, the event itself was nothing like what I had expected. What I remember most clearly is how *eerie* it all seemed. As the shadow moved across sun's face, the field in which we stood — which had been alive with the customary country sounds of birds and insects and cattle and tittering sisters — quietened, and the deep, rich greens and browns, the yellow of the primroses in the hedge-row — all paled, so that it felt as if we had gone, in a few moments, from midday to twilight.

And then the light returned, and with it vibrancy and sound.

That is how your absence makes me feel: as if the better half of the savour and colour has been leeched away and all is stale and pallid. "I have of late, but wherefore I know not," et cetaera.

I almost convinced myself to abandon Pemberley to go with them. Yet I know you shall return soon, though it does not seem soon enough for my faint heart. Too, I could hear my father's admonition at my parents' leaving Derbyshire — that he was glad that his giddiest remaining unmarried daughter should be safe with me at Pemberley, far from *soldiers* and from the *fleshpots of the South*. Poor Kitty.

Yet it was wonderful as always to hear from Jane. I spent much of the rainy morning answering her, begging her, if she were to see you in the capital, *not* to tell me of it, since I could not stand to hear of anyone enjoying your company when I cannot — but then begging that she write the moment she saw you to tell me how she found you.

Again, I am a fool. Yet I remain, I pray, *your* fool. I hope I continue to amuse you, goose that I am. If I am to be a goose, then, let me be a *prize* goose. The Prince Regent himself shall confer upon me the Order of the Silly Goose, and I and all our female descendants shall be honoured with the title Mother Goose.

I thought of sending this along with them, but Jane wrote that our mother had insisted that she and Charles stay in Hertfordshire some few days before continuing on to London, and so I judged that — if our trusty Cockney Cupid be steady on his rounds — my words would reach you more directly by his hand than should I have my sister and brother-in-law deliver it. Also, I believe that they may be, if it were possible, even more disgustingly in love than you and I, and while I do not doubt their love for you or me, nor their general dependability, I thought that perhaps entrusting the precious *billet doux* of one lovesick newlywed to the hands of two equally besmitten turtledoves might be courting, if not disaster, at the least a comedy of errors. And while you know that I love to laugh, I should prefer not to find that my letter to my lord and husband — and only the fifth that I have written as *Mrs. Darcy* — had gone astray. And so I shall wait for the rider's return (hopefully with fresh and incendiary words from you) to finish this and send it speeding southward.

The second letter that demanded my attention came — as you might have guessed — from Lady Malkin. I had rather hoped that, having hosted her here at Pemberley and having been hosted at Langley Park, I might reasonably have been able to avoid the lady's company (preferably for the rest of our natural lives), but she seems determined to plague me with her beauty, her *wiles and allurements,* and, as you shall see, her apparent disinterest in the appearance of propriety.

She wrote to say that Mr. Lackey had told Mr. Shelley of the excellent trout streams to be found on the grounds at Pemberley; she asked whether the gentlemen might fish there the next day — today, that is — and then, if they were welcome, might the lady and her children join me and my sisters for tea. Though I was pleased that she had at least *asked*, I was dismayed that I could think of no reasonable pretense for refusing. Since the post arrived while we were at breakfast, I even asked Georgiana and Kitty if they could think of a polite reason to demur without giving offense, but of course they were both *delighted* at the prospect of the younger Ginivers coming to visit.

If I were to ask Grouse to shoot and stuff the lady *after* she has requested entry, does the law stand on my side, Hon Mr. Justice of the Peace for the County? What would it say to monkshood or foxglove in her tea? Or would so gleefully murderous a course sail me far from the windy side o' the law?

I was afraid that it might, and so I wrote back and, as graciously as I could manage (grudging in mind though I hope not in tone), extended our hospitality, of both the grounds and the house.

I am, you will not be surprised to learn, *dreading* their visit. If I do not finish this letter, then she, or I, or both of us are dead. And since all of my worldly goods are yours already, I have only my spite to bestow upon Lady Malkin, in the event that she survive me.

Alas and hurrah, neither of us have died, and so I may finish this letter.

The full company arrived by a pair of carriages after the rain had cleared somewhat in the mid-afternoon — the lady, of course, along with the two poets, Lackey and Shelley (with all their tackle), the *ginger* Giniver siblings, and, naturally, the strangely saturnine Mary (whose surname I finally learned — but I shall tell you that later, since I do not wish to spoil my own surprise). I passed the gentlemen on to the care of the excellent Grouse, who promised to show them "the finest streams below the Peaks" and led them into the woods in the direction where you and Uncle Edward enjoyed the sport at just this time last year.

(Is the gamekeeper truly *Young* Grouse? He has a craggy, ageless look that makes me think that perhaps he has been keeping the woods and grounds here since the time of William the Conqueror. That his elder — and his mother! — should be living and breathing and telling tales seems a wonder!)

At Mrs. Reynolds's suggestion, I led the ladies (plus young Mr. Giniver — am I to call him *Lord Tommy*? No one has suggested so, yet I do not wish to appear uncouth to his mother) into the breakfast room, which has such a beautiful view over the lake and down into the valley. It served as a reminder to me (and, coincidentally, to our guests) that while Langley Park is lovely, it is not Pemberley. It may have been somewhat missish of me to take pleasure in so petty an aspect of so beautiful a prospect, but the glory of the view did leave me feeling far more ready to face Lady Malkin.

The conversation as we took tea remained at first light. Augustina and Georgiana fell into some discussion of *heat* and *drive.* I believe they were speaking of steam engines, but in all honesty I could not follow their discussion. Kitty played the coquette, as is her wont, and asked Mr. Giniver why he had not joined the men in their fishing? The young heir's fair skin darkened, which of course lead to all of the ladies — myself and his mother included — to tease the poor young man rather mercilessly. This was not kind of us, perhaps, but a cat who sets himself among such pigeons will be pecked.

(I seem to be foisting bird metaphors upon myself. Am I a pigeon or a goose?)

Only odd Mary remained silent.

Now, as I write this, it seems odd to me that we women all decided that young Master Giniver's discomfort was in any way a result of his romantic interest in or attachment to anyone. Indeed, thinking on it, Thomas has always struck me as a bit of a blank slate — hardly the young Romeo.

Yet that was the burden of our teasing: whom did he like, we wondered; what hearts had he broken, and who had broken his?

Kitty was the lead prosecutor in this trial by humiliation, but Augustina, Lady Malkin, and even Georgiana assisted her ably.

The poor object of their teasing sat glumly, legs and arms in an indecorous knot, attempting to parry their thrusts with the most monosyllabic of retorts.

I glanced to Mary, who seemed to be staring darkly out the windows. "Do romantic exploits not amuse you, Miss Mary?" When she fixed her steady, knowing gaze on me, I asked, "Are you not interested in matters of love?"

"I care a great deal about love," she said, mouth downturned. "It is Tommy I do not care for."

Since I had nothing to say on that subject, I did what I always seem to do, even when it is least appropriate. I teased her. I smiled my most wicked, Lizzy Bennet-ish smile and sang quietly, "My life upon 't, young though thou art, thine eye hath stay'd upon some favour that it loves."

The dour young women startled, then batted her eyes *at me,* and sang right back, "A little, by your favour." When that statement struck me speechless, her face returned to its habitual frown. "You *were* quoting *Twelfth Night,* were you not?"

"I — that is, yes," I stammered.

She frowned more deeply yet, and then nodded sagely. "Ah. You thought that I was expressing desire for *you.*"

It was then my turn to nod.

She answered my nod with another of her own, and then said, with great seriousness, "You are a very pretty woman, Mrs. Darcy, and an interesting one, and your eyes are quite exquisite, but you need not fear my fancy."

I assumed that she meant that she was taken with the *ginger swot,* Miss Giniver, but she leaned closer and disillusioned me. "Percy and I are deeply in love," she whispered fervently. "I shall marry him, shall bear his children, and shall continue to love him beyond death."

"I see," was all that I could say. And then, because, where her earlier statement had struck me dumb, this one apparently struck me insensible to tact, I asked, "Does it not bother you that Mr. Shelley has… spent so much time with your hostess, Lady Malkin?" I glanced to where the lady herself, our sisters, and Augustina all continued to torment young Thomas.

Mary waved the question away. "Percy and I believe that, to be given truly, love must be free."

"I see," I said once more, though I could in fact see very little. "You are, then, Godwinites?"

Whatever response I might have anticipated, a raucous peel of laughter from that forbidding young face came as an utter shock.

It was then that she told me that *of course* she is a Godwinite, since she is, in fact, the daughter not only of William Godwin, who has written so much on the subject of *free-love,* but also the daughter of the author of *Vindication of the Rights of Women,* which I am very pleased to see represented in the Pemberley library — and not in the restricted upper shelves, either! Odd Mary's name is indeed *Mary Wollstonecraft Godwin.*

My thoughts on the writings of Mary's parents I shall have to leave to another time — perhaps a much later time — since these thoughts will tend to roil, rather, and I do not feel myself fit to express them in anything like a reasoned fashion. I can say this much: I committed myself to marriage with you whole-heartedly and without reservation. My oaths at our wedding were made, not to the Lord Above, to the institution of marriage, to the Church of England, to the Rev. Mr. Whitley, to the assembled guests, nor even to you as my lord and husband, but to you as Fitzwilliam Henry Darcy, the man whom I love with all my silly heart. If you have any thoughts on the subject of marriage or the rights of women or free-love, I should be very pleased to hear them, since — beside that affirmation — my own are such a muddle, and, in any case, it always gives me pleasure to hear your thoughts.

I continued to talk with Mary, not about her parents nor her arrangement with Mr. Shelley, thankfully, but about the poetry of Shakespeare, and what she called the *breeches roles* — girls who dressed as men, such as Viola, Rosalind, Portia, and Imogen. (I believe she mentioned two or three others whom I had not even remembered.) Odd as she unquestionably is and downcast as her countenance may be, she is a fascinating conversationalist.

Soon after Mary's revelation, however, I found myself swept out of the breakfast room and into the grounds by Lady Malkin. She wished, she said, to visit the gentlemen as they fished, and begged my guidance. I attempted to demur, since I had, at best, only a vague notion of exactly where in the park Mssrs. Lackey and Shelley might be. Yet she insisted, and we set out in the direction where I had seen you lead my uncle just last summer.

I believe that it was on that day that I came to realise how deeply I had fallen in love with the gracious, honourable Gentleman Prince of Pemberley. And began to hope that perhaps your feelings for me were not altogether turned to hatred. Had news of Lydia not separated us, I wonder: should we have come together sooner? Or would we have danced politely about each other's feelings for even longer before confessing the truth to each other? I know that we have your aunt to thank, in many ways, for our marriage. Do you think my ungracious and dishonourable youngest sister delayed our bliss or hastened it? In either case, all's well that ends well. (Ah! Another of Miss Mary's intriguing observations: that Helena in that play takes on the role of the male in her relationship with her erstwhile, unworthy beloved, even as she keeps her *women's weeds*.)

As we walked, I feared that Lady Malkin would interrogate me about you, about our marriage, or about my parentage. To my surprise, she offered me, instead, a somewhat aggrieved precis of *her* biography, of her sheltered childhood as the elder daughter of an impoverished Austrian *grafen* (a kind of duchess, I think, but with a holding "smaller than the Langley kitchen gardens") and a London merchant. Somewhat bewildered yet happy not to be under attack, I listened in silence. She informed me that she had realised early that women have no power but their own allure, that love was our only battlefield, and the only way to win was to practice detachment and discipline. "One seldom acquires the qualities one does not believe necessary," she said, and went on to tell me that she undertook to acquire those qualities that would assure her success on the battlefield Love. She had first begun by attempting to seduce the only man she might safely experiment with, a French priest, by telling him in the confessional that she had "done *all that women do*" — though she yet had very little idea of what that *all* might be. "Yet," she said, "if an unfortunate woman should first feel the weight of her chains, what risks does she not run if she attempts to extricate herself from them, if she should dare to struggle against them?"

And so she had studied control of her own countenence and ways to see through men's (and other women's) and so to gain some control over them as well.

She proceeded to tell me how she had managed to enter her marriage with Lord Malkin still *virgo intacta,* though only technically so, how her marriage was loveless, since her husband was little present and, in any case, seemed to prefer the company of men and — she added with much emphasis though no apparent bitterness — of *young boys,* and so after they had consummated their marriage once, producing Thomas, they had not lain together again for some two years, during which time Lady Malkin resolved to continue her battle plan and began maneuvers. How she had spied one particularly delectable, particularly promising target in the son and heir of Pemberley, who was some few years her junior, and so had begun — she here shifted from military to hunting metaphors — to stalk him, studying how best to run him to ground.

As she began to tell this story while we walked, her gaze remained coquettishly upon me, waiting for my reaction.

I told her that you had told me of this — that we had no secrets between us, you and I.

She smiled, saying this was *most admirable,* and proceeded to dismiss the subject by saying that, once she had learned what she could from you and realised your limitations for sport, she had moved on to other game.

She laughed to see my indignation at her referring to your *limitations,* and said, "I am sure that he makes an *excellent* husband, my dear, all the more so for the skills that he and I learned together."

In truth my indignation was double — for I could not stand to hear her speak so dismissively of *you,* yet, if I am honest, I could not stand to hear her speak of you *at all.*

Oh, Darcy, I was not at *all* jealous to hear you tell me of your time with her. And yet hearing the lady speak of it as if it were naught but a bagatelle, a *nothing,* filled me with a jealous passion that left me all but speechless. How *dare* she speak of my husband, perfect and beautiful, as if he were of no account?

I was aware too that this was precisely the response Lady Malkin sought to evoke, though I could not nor cannot imagine why, and so I did my best to hold my tongue.

We were some distance into the woods, and I will admit that in following Lady Malkin's tale I had rather lost any sense of where we were. We came across the figure of a straight-backed woman, hair stark white, digging with a stick at the base of a tree — poking at what I came to recognise as mushrooms.

"Good day, Mother Grouse," called my companion.

The woman looked up, her face lined but handsome, and peered at us. "Ay'up, young 'Lizbett," she answered Lady Malkin. Then she shifted her grey-green gaze to me. "And thee'll be t'new Mistress Darcy. Ha'thee."

Taking that for a greeting, I nodded and answered, "It is a pleasure to meet you, Mrs. Grouse. My husband has told me much about you."

She gave me a knowing smile. "Aye, young Willy will ha'told thee o'us." She leaned upon her stick. "But ah denna think thee'll be in need o'our services yet."

"Services?" I asked, pleased that I had followed her speech even so far, but mostly pleased by her name for you. Young Willy! I shall call you that at every opportunity, I believe. I shall introduce you to every guest at our home and to every stranger we meet upon the road as *my husband, young Willy.* When we disport ourselves and you cause me to call out, it shall be "Oh, just *there,* young Willy!" that I scream. All of these thoughts raced through my silly head, and yet it was confusion about her mention of *services* that apparently showed upon my face.

Mrs. Grouse smiled broadly and Lady Malkin laughed. The noblewoman bowed to the old woman and said, "Mother Grouse is the finest midwife in the district."

"Oh, aye," said Mrs. Grouse, a white eyebrow raised. "And a healer and all."

"Oh!" I said, "Darcy told me you were nurse to him and his sister!"

"Aye," she said nodding. "And two such sweet babes we ne'er did see. 'Sides our own, 'course. Now, what brings'ee twain out t'woods?"

I answered, "We are looking for two gentlemen whom your son brought out to fish."

"Oh, aye," said Mrs. Grouse with another nod. "They's down the track a short ways." She pointed with her stick along the path that we had been following. "Come t'fork and bear'ee right, and thee'll come on'em soon, so."

I thanked her, and then, before we continued on our way, I asked, "And how are you certain that I am not — that I do not yet need your services?"

Her smile broadened, "'Tis plain to see, lass. Thee'll bear'im babes soon 'nough, fear no'. But no' yet."

"Oh," I said, not convinced, but disappointed nonetheless. "And... were you looking for mushrooms?" Hill had taken us out into the woods between Longbourn and the Lucases' house to search for what she called *chicken o'the woods*, a bright orange mushroom that she loved to add to her lamb stews.

"Oh, aye," said Mrs. Grouse, nodding once more. "See tha'?" with her stick she pointed at three large, broad-brimmed mushrooms that were pushing up from the dirt. "See they tops? They look like penny buns or such as thy young Mary Patchett calls *Ceps*, as makes good eatin'. But they's no' brown, see, they's greenish. 'Tis hard t'see i't'shadows, but right 'nough, they's green. And see they's stems? How they's skinny, wi' tha' cup, like, at bottom? And they." She took her stick and tipped the top of one mushroom, revealing a frill beneath. "They gills. Tha's the final sign. They's death caps."

"Oh," said both Lady Malkin and I.

"Aye. 'Twould kill any fool so much as tasted'em."

"Goodness," I said. "Shouldn't we dispose of them?"

"Oh, aye?" the old woman laughed, yet she did not sound at all amused. "And how would'st do tha'? Pick they and put they in compost and they'll grow. Burn they and the smoke'll make'ee sick." She grimaced. "Our Silas'll come and bury they. Tha'll keep any foolish young kitchen maids — or they's ladies — fro' doing nowt mutton-headed."

"Who is Silas?" I asked, though my mind was on serving Lady Malkin a mushroom pie.

"Our son," she clucked. "Him as ye call *Young Grouse*."

It hadn't occurred to me to ask his Christian name, the more mutton-headed me.

Lady Malkin and I bid her good day, and continued on our way. My companion seemed lost in thought, and I was considering the conversation, and how Mrs. Grouse's colourful rusticity seemed to hide a genuine shrewd-ness, when something from the very beginning of our meeting struck me. I turned to Lady Malkin and asked whether her name was indeed Elizabeth.

"Indeed," she replied. "Another thing we seem to share." She wrinkled her pretty nose. "No one calls me that now. My mother called me *Liesel.* My husband does me the honour of calling me *Lady Malkin* — even in pri-vate. Some of my lovers have called me *Eliza* or *Lizzy.* It amuses young Miss Godwin to call me *Betsy.*"

"On what occasion?"

"Well, if I am to play with the pretty Mr. Shelley, she *will* join in, of course."

Even knowing that she had meant to shock me, I was yet abashed by her candor. Even so, I managed to say, "And what should you like me call you, Lady Malkin?"

She laughed. "Ah, well done! I should have expected you to be too ap-palled by that even to continue our conversation. *Brava!* Perhaps, if it content you, we may call one another *Elizabeth,* since I see we shall be great friends?"

"Certainly, Elizabeth." I am not certain why I accepted the familiarity. I do not like the woman — though her story certainly gave me reason to consider my prejudice against her. I do not trust her — and her story had given me no new reason to do so. Yet clearly we shall be much in each other's company, whether I will or no, and so perhaps it is best that I treat her as a friend, even when we both know that she is none.

In any case, we soon reached the place on the stream where the two poets, Lackey and Shelley, had been fishing. They were stowing away their gear as we approached.

"Ladies!" called Mr. Shelley, shaking his head as he gave us a bow, so that his flowing locks caught the sunlight that lanced between the tree limbs. "We were just now speaking of how it was time to put aside childish things, and turn to lovely ladies, la, and love."

"Ah, Mr. Shelley," cooed Lady Malkin, "very poetic!" She took his hand. "Mrs. Darcy, *Elizabeth,* would you mind if Mr. Shelley and I were to take a stroll through these lovely woods and take in the sunset?"

With as careless an air as I could affect, I bowed my head and said, "Of course, *Elizabeth.* The skies seem to have cleared. It should be a lovely evening for a walk. After, if you should care to dine with us, we would be delighted for you to join us."

As she and Mr. Shelley skipped off into the woods, Mr. Lackey fixed me with an unsentimental, rather careworn grin. "Will you lead me back to the house, Mrs. Darcy? I am afraid that Shelley has left me with all of the gear — and the fish — and so I could do with some assistance, with some direction, and of course, with the pleasure of your company."

"It would be my pleasure, Mr. Lackey. Lend me the creel." When he began to object to my taking the fish hamper, I tutted, "I am a daughter of the country, Mr. Lackey. I have helped birth lambs and slaughter chickens. I can carry some trout."

He bowed with a flourish and handed me the creel, which, though properly malodorous, felt rather light. As he gathered up the rods and other tools of the angler's art, he shrugged. "We did not catch much, though there were fish aplenty. Shelley will be talking."

I laughed, made some inane comment about *poets, lovers, and madmen,* and we set off back toward the house.

"I am surprised," said Mr. Lackey as we trudged along, "to see you and Lady Malkin on such companionable terms — if you do not mind my saying so, Mrs. Darcy."

"Oh, you are no more surprised than I, Mr. Lackey. When I woke this morning, if you had told me that the lady and I would be calling each other by our given names before the sun set, I should have thought you mad or mendacious."

"Yes," said the tutor. "Lady Malkin… is an acquired taste. And not one frequently cultivated by other ladies, in my experience."

"No, I can see that. And have *you* acquired such a taste, Mr. Lackey?" It was, perhaps, a bit forward of me, and yet my time with the lady herself must have eroded my already limited tact.

He frowned and shook his head. "My tastes run… elsewhere. Yet the lady has, from time to time, expressed a taste for *Lackey,* and I…"

"And you are not in a position to say no to such a lady. I understand." And I did — for how was he to deny her, any more than George Wickham might have done all those years ago?

We walked in silence for some time, until Pemberley itself rose before us. As we prepared to step into the house, he stopped and said, "Please, Mrs. Darcy, do not judge her too harshly. Lady Malkin is a woman of talents completely wasted on her station and circumstances. She has the kind of ruthless intellect that would have made her a brilliant general, were she a man, and yet she must spend her days presiding over a country house in dresses of silk and lace. I think she might have been happier and better suited had she been lower-born and less beautiful. As it is, the world expects naught from her, now that she has produced the customary heir and a spare, but to be decorous and gay."

"The world, I think, expects a certain amount of propriety, Mr. Lackey, but I am not the world, and I will do my best to follow your admonition and reserve judgment. However, I will tell you that any ill will I may bear her proceeds from disapproval, not of her behaviour, but of her lack of consideration for the feelings of others. Her use of you yourself, it seems, might stand as evidence of her disregard for others' feelings."

"As you say, Mrs. Darcy," granted Mr. Lackey, and then we entered the house.

I delivered the dozen or so trout to *young Mary Patchett's* kitchens, and asked that indomitable lady and Mrs. Reynolds if the Langley Park party might join us at supper. They both smiled that I had asked, and informed me that they had planned on just such an eventuality, down to the fresh-caught trout as part of the fish course.

Dinner was a lively affair, especially once Lady Malkin and Mr. Shelley returned, just as the sun finished setting. Though they looked somewhat windswept, they did not give any direct evidence of those activities in which I was certain they had engaged. Indeed, the lady smiled at me as she sat to my right, and *apologised* that she had worn no *pearls* to dinner.

I answered that she herself would be the brightest jewel at any table, a witticism that seemed to please her.

After a wonderful meal — and Mrs. Patchett's presentation of the trout was truly delicious — Lady Malkin ordered her carriage. Her children, however, begged to spend the evening at Pemberley, as, to my surprise, did Miss Mary. The mother granted her permission (contingent upon mine, which I happily granted) and then she and the two poets departed.

I will confess that I felt as if I had withstood a siege. Your chatelaine has kept the enemy from ransacking the castle, and has driven her from the gates, my lord.

When next she comes, it may yet come to mushroom pie, or pistols at ten paces, or fingernails at arms' length. Yet I am relieved to have lived to fight another day.

I retired to the library to write this account of my rather ridiculous day for you. Now that I have written it, I am both amused and appalled at its length and serendipity.

Too, I am saddened by the relative lack of *wifely musings,* which I must assure you have been incessant, but were not germane to the tales I wished to spin for you.

And of course, just as I was about to begin to share those musings at *length* and in *detail,* the young people — guests and sisters — have descended upon me here in the library.

Georgiana and Augustina were all apology, asking whether their presence would disturb me, but I assured them that, no, I welcomed their company, and that I was merely sharing my report of the day with my husband. All of the young ladies thought this was rather sweet. I am glad that I did not say anything about how I wish that you were here, for me to suck your cock into my mouth and feel it swell there.

And I am likewise glad that I was able to write that at the bottom of a page, and so leave peering eyes nothing to gaze upon.

Yet know that I *weep* for you, though my eyes are dry.

Georgiana asks when we should expect our courier. I have told her that, by my calculations (undertaken on an hourly basis since he departed Derbyshire), we should expect him at the earliest tomorrow midday (although I secretly hope that he shall arrive much sooner).

Augustina has prevailed upon Georgiana to play, which is delightful as always. Tommy seems to have invited Kitty to take a stroll about the room, which she has readily accepted, with many giggles and much fluttering of eyelashes.

It makes me think, I will confess, of Miss Caroline Bingley's promenade with me about the sitting room at Netherfield. Who, I wonder, is Master Giniver's intended audience, or does he simply wish to have Kitty to himself? I know now for a fact that neither your sister, nor his, nor odd Miss Godwin would wish to trade places with her, so perhaps it is that.

Both Miss Giniver and odd Mary have begun to use the nickname of *Gigi* for your sister, to both our sisters' apparent delight.

The four young women are conversing in French, which Kitty knows I cannot speak, confound her. Mary seems to have retrieved a book — the same green-covered book as before, I believe, though from where I do not know — and has begun to read from it. They all are listening, quite rapt, and I find I am cursing *myself* now, and my own lack of skill with languages. I can discern the word *amour* quite frequently, which I can credit, since the book *is* French. Yet it irks me that they are reading something with such evident interest, and I have no inkling of what the subject may be, unless it be that it touches on love.

You must return, Darcy, and bless me with your gift of tongues. Oh, I am most open to such a lesson now, and wish —

Goodness. Our Cupid has just arrived. He is just as disheveled and besmirched with road dust. I shall

Well, then, I have taken my leave of all and retreated with your letter to our bedchamber. Our wonderful, smutty courier I bade visit me in the library tomorrow morning to take my reply to you; I gave him into the care of our sisters, and enjoined them to see him well fed and quartered, which they, gigglingly, promised to do.

I could not wait to get myself alone with your letter. Florry, who saw our courier's arrival, was waiting for me in the room, *almost* smiling, rather than the severe pout that she has been wont to wear of late, and helped me out of my gown. When she asked if I needed her assistance in any other way, I said no, and shooed her out of the room with only slightly less than brute force.

Oh, my dearest, sweetest Darcy! Your letter! I was already *weeping* with desire when I opened it, and in reading it — and reading it again — I *overflowed* with all of the love and ardor that you inspire in me.

The world has colour and savour once more.

In answer to your last postscript but one, I shall mark this paper with my own passion, drawn from the very depths of me:

[Discolouration]

I hope that my *mark* shall inspire you as yours has inspired me. Smell, I have always found, is a powerful sense for unlocking memory. Though it be but a phantasm, the scent on yours returns you to me, just as I would have you (unclothed and at the ready). Know that my spot above contains within it the whole globe's worth of my desire for you. I am here, naked and willing. Smell it, come, and take me.

Your thoughts on how your experiences with *our good friend Elizabeth Giniver* have coloured our marriage strangely echo my own. Clearly we are of a mind.

And yet you persist in speaking of the *consequences* of those experiences, in spite of my having assured you — and I will assure you again — that nothing that you have told me that you and she did over a decade before you met me troubles me in the slightest. Your persistence, alas, makes me worry that there is yet something that you have not shared with me.

Is this the case? If so, please, Darcy, share it with me, and I promise I shall forgive you, and then we may lay the whole business to rest.

Speaking of business, what is it that you are up to with my uncle (or rather, as you properly say, *our* uncle) Gardiner? Is it too much for me to ask? I do not wish to intrude, and yet I must confess myself intrigued by what business you two may have been engaged in. If I am prying, please let me know. I shall not take it ill, I promise, though I may pout.

We must clearly read Mr. Donne's poems together! I find that the idea of you reading his thoroughly beautiful, thoroughly indecent elegy *To His Mistress on Going to Bed* to me while we are together in *our* bed is a most delightful and inspiring one. Am I your *America?* Your *new found land?*

As to the works of Mssrs. Coleridge and Blake — I hope that I may show you some of the reasons that I love their poems. Also, as libertine as Mr. Coleridge may present himself in his poems, may I ask whether you have ever read his essays, especially those on the works of Shakespeare (essays that Miss Mary and I discussed in passing this afternoon)? If you do not find them worth reading on their own account, perhaps I can offer you some reward for having read them?

Odd, *interesting* Miss Mary is in fact somewhat younger than Georgiana I believe. She may indeed be younger than Lydia, a thought that I should rather not dwell on, given what I know about both young women. Should Mary Godwin be my younger sister rather than Lydia Wickham, I should be happy for far more stimulating conversation. However, her morals are no more conventional (though at least rather more researched).

And yes, Miss Giniver does deserve the title of *most interesting*. Intelligence — as opposed to *wit* — is a virtue little prized in women, as Mr. Lackey implied with regards to Augustina's mother. Yet I believe that I can say that I have never met anyone — man or woman — more curious, more gifted with insight, or more excited by the world about her. I find her, if I may be so bold, humbling. That Georgiana manages to hold her own in their conversations on matters of natural philosophy does her great credit. I am not sure that there are many who could.

Do I have cause to be jealous of the *ginger-headed swot?* Shall I have to keep her from you — or must I study the teachings of Mssrs. Newton, Linnaeus, and Watt to hold my place in your esteem?

I hope not, for I had rather hoped that I might confine my field of study for the near future to bettering my skill at *tongues*.

(I shall not tire of jests on that theme for some time, I am afraid.)

(Oh, how I look forward to the feel of your tongue — clapper, red rag, et cetaera — upon my jewel — pussy, cleft of joy, Venerable Monosyllable, et cetaera. I wish that you were here now. I am quite naked, but for a cloth beneath my et cetaera, et cetaera to keep from soaking the seat. And yet there is no one but myself to give me the release for which I ache, and so relieve myself I must, poor me. Oh, how I wish you were here to taste me! I wish you could taste every part of me, and I you! Perhaps we could pleasure each other so at the same time, like two snakes, each swallowing the other's tail? I should like to try that, Darcy. I should like to try it *now,* alas!)

Yes, my husband, your debauched and bibliophilic wife has read the adventures of that most dissolute heroine, Fanny Hill. I found her tale highly *educational,* though in looking back, I can see that I understood very little of what she encountered.

And since all five of the Bennet sisters have already at least *glanced* at that *most accomplished in vulgarity of English novels*, I do not think that Papa need extend his bookshelves. The horse has already, as the Hertfordshire farmers like to say, left the barn.

It delights me to hear that you are delighted by my voice when moved by passion (as you so skillfully move me). Your voice upon reaching the little death is a wonder to me as well — deep and low as a bull's bellow, and yet sweet and gentle, as Bottom tells us of his lion's roar.

The last morning, when I took your Upstanding Member in my Parliamentary organ (though never before was parliament conducted in the bath, I should think), as I brought you to release, I found that my own fingers had found my et cetaera, et cetaera. When you bellowed at last, and spilled yourself onto my waiting tongue — and onto my chin and cheek — your cry was the impetus that sent me, too, over the cliff and into my own little death.

Oh, Darcy, I long to hear that bellow again. I long to taste you. I long to *feel you inside of me.*

How can I continue to live, to walk, to breathe, without you here to bring me to such bliss? I shall die, I fear, and the death shall not be a little one.

I feel for poor Harrison. I hope that you, like me, might take to reading my letters *as God made you.* Not only would that save your valet much labour, but the image of you receiving my words unclothed delights me more than I can say.

And yes — I shall kiss you upon your *artistic* bum at the earliest opportunity, and you shall see why I so delight in your doing so to me.

I shall accept that you find me lovely on the condition that you accept that I find you so.

Accept that, and fuck my cunt with your cock as often as it please you. And I do hope that it shall please you to do so until I am as white-haired as Mrs. Grouse.

I shall ask Kitty whether she remembers the game of Tom o' Straw any better than I do. I believe that it was one of those games that was the more entertaining, the larger the number of assembled players. The more I try to remember the rules of the game, the more befuddled I find I become. I am not altogether certain that utter chaos was not the intended end of the game.

I am also not entirely sure that some of the older boys and girls necessarily remained fully clothed while playing it. My sisters and I certainly never engaged in any *country matters* during the game, of that I *am* sure, not even Lydia, nor did Charlotte and Maria Lucas. But as I now remember it, some of the older players would from time to time disappear — and often in pairs. I wonder that I never noticed that at the time. I shall see if Kitty's recollection matches mine, and if she has a clearer memory of the rules, if indeed it had any.

In any case, I should delight altogether in playing such a game with the upstanding Master of Pemberley. I am glad to hear, too, that you are no puritan, and look forward to proving it with you.

Thank you for making clear what I should have done with Miss Lewis! I know that I had no way of guessing that I should have done so, yet I feel some small shame for not having simply asked Mrs. Patchett or the Reynoldses. I shall consult with them tomorrow.

It is now past midnight. On the one hand, it is late, and I regret spending so much of my day in writing to you when I could simply have ridden to London and leapt into your arms. I have just counted, and my letter has now run to over twenty-three pages front and back! Any longer and it should be a novel, and a tiresome one. Poor Junkets, our Cockney Cupid, shall have to hire another horse simply to carry my envelope.

On the other hand, it is now the twenty-first, and so one day closer to your riding back to me. And how can that make me anything but happy?

I shall sleep now — or try to — and meet with our courier in the library tomorrow morning.

With adorations, fertile tears, with groans that thunder love, with sighs of fire, yours,

Elizabeth Anne Bennet Darcy

PS I came into the library to find Junkets already here, with Georgiana attending him (and Kitty, of all people, playing the chaperone). He was admiring the books with loud, puppyish excitement. I told him that I needed to read over this letter before sealing it, and so he should feel free to examine any of the volumes. When he asked which, I suggested the copy of Chapman's Homer that I have been reading, which was upon the table at his side. With great pleasure, he sat (he is clean, this morning, thank goodness), opened the volume, and began to read it in his broad London accent to our two sisters — to Georgiana's polite delight and Kitty's amusement. EABD

PPS I think your sister might appreciate a letter from her brother. Not only would it give her pleasure to hear from you, but it would give young Junkets a chance to speak with her about something other than our house or the ride from London. And I believe they would both enjoy that conversation. Your letters being less longwinded than mine, we might as well take advantage of the ready courier, might we not? EABD

PPPS I shall write my aunt Gardiner. I had meant to do so last night, but for some reason my thoughts were caught up with other matters. I cannot think why. EABD

PPPPS I shall continue to see whether I can uncover the French author who has so captured the attention of such disparate imaginations as Georgiana Darcy, Kitty Bennet, Augustina Giniver, and Mary Godwin.

PPPPPS I am relieved to hear that you never seriously considered marrying either Charles's sister nor your cousin. I am somewhat surprised and amused that you attempted to play Cupid between Anne and your friend, however. Did you really think such a marriage likely? I had always assumed that you had entertained hopes for Charles and your sister. EABD

PPPPPPS Florry has just come in with my breakfast, which I had neglected to eat, and has collapsed into tears — most unlike her. Kitty, Georgiana, and even Junkets are all trying to comfort her, but to no avail. I shall seal this letter with no other trace of passion than my kiss, and endeavour to discover what is causing her such distress. EABD

Aside – Riding on a Pony

From Elizabeth Darcy to Margaret Gardiner

Pemberley, Derbyshire, *August 22*

My dearest aunt Margaret,

I have been most thoughtless in failing to answer your letter of congratulations after the wedding. Your words were kindness itself, and your presence (along with that of uncle Edward, as well as my ever-delightful young cousins) was one of the high points of the wedding.

Alas, as you suggested, I have been rather distracted of late. I cannot think why.

Well, of course, I can indeed think why, and I will not be coy, since your letter so sensibly eschewed coyness: I have the most beautiful, attentive husband in the world.

As to your very practical questions regarding our compatibility, oh, allow a giddy, enraptured girl to assure you that we have found that we are very *well-matched in harness* indeed. We have discovered so through daily and — it sometimes seems — hourly experimentation. To date, we have yet to find anything that might give one of us pleasure that does not give the other pleasure as well.

And thank you for your *most helpful* suggestions! The proposal, in particular, that I take him between what he and I have taken lately and laughingly to calling my *mounts pleasant* was a particular rousing success. I did not, when I blushingly read your receipt for the action, believe that I had enough available to me to press around him so, and yet experience proved me a fool.

Alas, as you most likely know (since I know my uncle will have told you), my husband was forced to attend to business in London this last fortnight of August, and I have been left with naught but his letters and occasional visits from more or less welcome guests from the county to keep me warm. Kitty is here, and my new sister-in-law, and their company has been welcome. Yet I have found that Darcy's absence fills me with a despondency I have few weapons to combat. I have found myself pouring my benighted soul into letters to my husband — and pouring over his letters to me. And I will thank you to withhold surmise over the contents of those letters, since I know you know very well their burden.

The canker that is currently gnawing at my bud comes from his letters to me, and I hope that you do not mind that I unburden myself to you.

I knew, when we married, that Darcy had been *intimate* with women before we met. He was most forthright about it, as he seems to be in all things, and most apologetic. I told him then, and have told him again, that I did not mind, that I was happy that at least one of us had some working knowledge of what to do and needn't rely solely on the practical lessons provided by a very helpful aunt.

Unfortunately, circumstances have conspired to reveal to me the lady with whom he gained that *working knowledge*. And while I continue to hold to my equanimity as best I can, a small blossom of jealousy has taken root in my heart, and I cannot seem to pluck it out.

The lady is older, and beautiful, and a peeress — sophisticated, witty, and urbane where I am unpolished, course, and altogether a raw country girl, a bumpkin. She has been most insistent, of late, that we be *great friends,* and such is her insistence that I have hardly been able to think how to repel her. I will admit, too, that I was fascinated to see what it was that my husband found alluring, albeit when he was not yet sixteen.

Now, however, I find that I am thinking of her and Darcy, of what they did together. Visions of their *carnal embraces* fill my mind at unattended moments, as I am walking in the beautiful grounds here, or reading in the library, or falling asleep in the bed in which I have, myself, enjoyed those very embraces with my beautiful, virtuous husband.

Darcy is extremely forthright — as I have said, he is so in every matter — that he has no tender feelings for the lady, nor yet any attraction to her. Indeed, he expresses outright loathing, and swears to me he has refused to be alone with her since the end of their liaison. He has sworn that what he enjoyed with her as compared to what he and I have enjoyed together was as a rush candle to a bonfire.

And yet jealousy grows.

There is something in what he has told me that makes me certain that I have not yet heard all — that there is some *consequence* of their brief arrangement that he has not yet shared with me, forthright though he may be.

I have done my best to avoid allowing the disease growing in my heart from leaking into my letters — I have done my best to assure him that I do not care about the past, especially as he was himself hardly responsible for his own actions (he was, I believe, of the age of Lydia, this past, tumultuous summer). Yet it is all that I can do not to cry when I see the lady (as I did just yesterday — and there is a story I shall share another time!) or to forbid her presence in our house or to fall into hysteria and write long letters of complaint to my husband. And yet I feel that if I were to allow myself to do any of those things, I should be giving the lady precisely what she wishes most (though why she wishes it, I cannot guess), and so I withhold my tears, my rage, and my bitter remonstrations.

The tutor to the lady's daughter, a poet named Lackey, told me yesterday that he believed that she should have been much happier and better-suited had she been born less beautiful — or had she been born a man. He said that she had the sort of *ruthless intelligence* that would have made her a great general — a trait that, coupled with her beauty, makes her most unpopular with other ladies, even as it (the beauty, at least) makes her most welcome among the gentlemen.

Even knowing that she has begun some sort of campaign against me and Darcy, knowing that she is laying siege to Pemberley, I find that I cannot think how to counter her. This is a lady whose whole life has, she has told me herself, been the study of the war-game of love and polite conversation. I feel woefully out of my depth, and all the more furious for it.

I do not fear for dear Darcy's affection, not truly. And I do not know what advice I could possibly ask from you, dear aunt, since the maneuvers of such a coquette as this are carried out in parlors far grander than those that you and I are accustomed to at Longbourn or in Gracechurch Street. Yet I must unburden myself to someone, and I fear I cannot do so to anyone but you, for which I once more apologise. My mother's response would be of such intemperate fury that I should end up having to care for *her*, and my sisters would be of no help either, wonderful as they all are. (Can you imagine what Mary would say in response to such a letter as I am writing you? I should receive a thick homily of great passion on the Evils of the World and the Lessons of Temptation, densely cross-referenced with quotes from the Bible, from St. Augustine, and from Fordyce's *Sermons*. The very thought makes me laugh, even as I miss her desperately.)

In any case, I hope that all is well there. Perhaps you have seen my husband? If so, I need not tell you not to betray any of what I have written here — I know you would not, yet the illness takes me so that I must ask in any case. I wrote to Jane, when she told me that she and Charles were off to London, and begged her that should she see my husband, she must not tell me of it, since I should be consumed with envy that she might bask in his presence when I was denied that pleasure. I will not so play the silly, love-sick girl with you — though you know me to be both silly and sick with love (among other things, it seems) — but will instead beg that you tell me how you find him. I fear that he is not caring for himself there in smoky, dirty, wonderful London, that he is working too hard, taking too little rest, and not eating well. Perhaps you can feed him for me?

My best to dear uncle Edward, and to Joan, Freddie, Billy, and Eddie, with many kisses and promises of pony rides when next they come to Derbyshire. (Though I think my uncle would look most comical on a pony!)

Your loving niece,

Elizabeth Anne Bennet Darcy

PS I take far too much delight in signing my new name. Does one ever get used to it? I pray not. EABD

10 – Hateful Confession

From Fitzwilliam Darcy to Elizabeth Darcy

Nr 12, Berkeley Sqr
London
August 23

My Dearest Mrs. Darcy,

I dined with both Mr. Kite, my factor, and with our uncle Edward this evening, celebrating what we hope to be the conclusion of one of the pieces of business that drew me from your side to London. We toasted your good health, and both men asked to be remembered to you.

There is but one more piece of business here that I wish to conclude — and Mr. Gardiner is aiding me with that as well. It is, I will tell you this much, an enterprise that I hope will delight you. But beyond saying that much, I will keep it a surprise. I hope that you will like it.

As the three of us were out and about in the town today, I found myself thinking of places that might give you delight here. While I am always happiest when home in Derbyshire, and while you have told me that you are a country girl through and through (a country *woman* now, I can aver), yet as we drove about London, I could not but consider all of the wonders and delights of this metropolis that we might share together: the theaters, the exhibitions, the balls, Westminster, St Paul's, and, of course, St James's. I know that we are, neither of us, as sociable as some. Yet I know too that both of us could enjoy society, so long as we had each other's company. Even the parks, which are, of course, nothing to the beauties of the countryside in which we are blest to live, have a comparatively quiet beauty that puts the bustle of the town in greater relief. I should love to show you the wonders of the city with which I am familiar, and explore together those with which I am not.

Our sister Jane has written to inform me that she and Bingley will soon be in London after a brief detour to Hertfordshire. I was delighted to hear that I shall see them before I ride north once more, but sad to know that they would be visiting without you.

I have grown to love your eldest sister very dearly. As I have come to know her, in all her native reticence and gentle consideration, the shame of my earliest impressions of her — and of the actions that I took with regards to those impressions — strike me deeply. I fear that I took her shyness for Lady Malkin's calculation, an unpardonable mistake. The only consolations are knowing how happy she and Bingley now are, in spite of my meddling, and how you have forgiven me, for which I shall eternally be grateful.

In any case, love Jane and Charles as I do, it is hard to think that I shall see them before I am graced to see you.

I will to bed early tonight, I think, and hope to dream of you — in all your unveiled glory. I hope that I shall visit your dreams as well. If we may not enjoy each other in the flesh, then let us do so in dreams. ~~Good night, my love.~~

Our wonderful Cockney Cupid has just arrived, quite wet and saddle-sore, it seems, but cheerfully carrying your letter, and all thoughts of sleep and bed are quite out of my head. I have sent him off to Mrs. McCartney, the Irish cook whom Mrs. Martin has engaged — though she is no Mrs. Patchett, she has proven a very capable cook, and I am sure that she will stuff young Junkets full to bursting. I told him to visit me in the morning to get my reply to you.

"Tender is the night! And haply the Queen-Moon is on her throne," he called, and left me alone with your *very* long letter, which I shall now read as slowly as I can bear to do, though I hunger to devour it all at once.

Indeed, a long letter, and a full one, and I have so many things to say in answer to what you have written, but first let me say how much I love and honour you.

Next, let me warn you never to take anything that Elizabeth Giniver says to you at face value. I know that you already know this, yet I can see in your telling of your encounter with her that she is doing her best to work upon you. What she hopes to gain, I cannot tell, and so I can only warn you to be wary of her, and of everything she may say or do.

While some portions of what she told you fit with what I know of her and her history, there are some parts of her tale that seem unlikely. Her birth I believe she reported to you accurately. I met Lady Sophia, her mother, and Mr. Desmond, her merchant father, at their daughter's wedding to Lord Malkin. I was truly a boy at the time, but I did believe that both mother and daughter were quite beautiful. (I was not to behold true beauty until I met you, of course, but as you say, *ignorance cannot know what it does not know.*)

Though I cannot be certain, however, there are other elements of her purported history that ring, if not *false*, then at least *less than perfectly true.* The exchange with her confessor, for example, does not have the complete air of verisimilitude to it.

As for her off-handed dismissal of Lord Malkin, and his purported appetites, I have heard her make those claims before, and while I cannot categorically deny them, I can stake my honour on their being, at the least, exceedingly unlikely.

When I was at school, I learned to recognise those of the boys who sought more than friendly companionship. One of my and Bingley's best friends there, William, was quite happily frank about his preference for the company of others of our sex, rather than of yours — as happy as Miss Godwin seems to be about her *lack* of preference. And one of our teachers was notorious for pursuing students — particularly the young and unwary. We all learned to know when his attention was upon us. We all learned never to go alone to his chambers.

I tell you all of this for two reasons — first to assure you that I am not unaware that there are some older men who like to prey upon young boys (and upon young girls too, of course).

Next, and most importantly, I wish to assure you that I have never seen any evidence that Lord Malkin is one of those men.

I have known the man literally all of my life. He was a friend of my father's, and a regular guest at Pemberley, even as I (and later Georgiana) were made welcome at Langley Park. I was alone with him on many occasions. I have seen him in the company of many young boys and men. And I have never seen any impropriety in his actions toward them, nor have I ever had any sense, such as said that I developed at school, of his amorous intent, whether directed at me or toward *anyone else*.

And that is the third thing that I wish to tell you about August Giniver, Lord Malkin: he is, I must assure you, the least amorous person I have ever known.

I do not mean to say that he is unpleasant or unkind; rather, he is uniformly and unerringly polite. However, I have never seen him show the slightest sign of any lascivious intent at all, whether toward a boy, a girl, a man, or a woman. In that regard I will most definitely include his wife. I can, with honesty, say that, when he first brought her into the district, Lord Malkin was the only male person I knew who did *not* show some such signs toward her.

When she and I were conducting our *assignations*, it was a theme to which she returned frequently in her complaint: that aside from consummating their marriage, he had treated her no differently than any other member of the household. It was then that she proceeded to make vague accusations along the lines that she made with you: that he was a seducer of young boys.

My father used to say of his friend that he spent all of his heart that might have gone toward amatory pursuits upon his passion for maintaining and improving his estate, and on hunting. In the whole of my experience with Lord Malkin, I have never seen any sign from him to contradict that observation.

He seems very fond of his children (Augustina most especially), and has always behaved fondly toward Lady Malkin. Toward everyone else — regardless of sex, of age, or of class — I have seen him behave with a polite disinterest.

It amused my father that his friend married one of the most famed beauties in the country, but almost as an afterthought. In all of their acquaintance (and they had known one another since boyhood) my father never heard his friend August express a romantic passion toward anyone or anything. When Lord Malkin brought Lady Elizabeth to Langley Park, my father congratulated him on having finally found love, and with such a lovely creature. Lord Malkin responded, "I suppose it is so. I will grant that she is pretty, and frightfully witty. In all honesty, I suppose I knew I needs must marry someone, as you and everyone else had kept telling me, and she seemed as likely a prospect as any."

I can show you the letter, if you care to see it.

I cannot say with certainty that Lord Malkin has *never* engaged in any such acts. *Absence of proof is no proof of absence,* &c. However, I can with some assurance label Lady Malkin's accusations toward her husband as highly unlikely at best and slanderous at worst.

That a person of such appetites as Lady Malkin should find herself married to a man who so lacks them — that is an irony that I will grant borders on the diabolical. However successful their marriage may seem by all outward signs, I must grant that it must be an absolute purgatory for her. I would almost feel sorry for her, did I believe that the experience had taught her anything but bitterness.

All of which is once again to put you on your guard with the lady.

And here is the point at which I must at last bare my most shameful secret to you — one that is not truly a secret, I suppose, but rather a secret fear.

You said that you sensed in my letter that I was not telling you all, that there was some *consequence* of my intercourse with Elizabeth Giniver that I had not yet fully shared with you.

And in your letter I see that the lady herself has begun to hint to you — as she has done to me, on those occasions when we have been pressed together in company — of that consequence.

It is this: I fear that Augustina, my sister's good friend, and our father's friend's favourite, may be in fact not his daughter, but mine.

I have never spoken those fears to a soul, Lizzy. I have scarcely dared to acknowledge them in my waking mind.

If so, the reality of such a betrayal would fill me with unbearable shame, even as the thought that I had any part in creating such a remarkable young creature sparks a peculiar kind of pride in me.

Therefore, no, Lizzy, you need not be jealous of *ginger swots*. I look on Miss Giniver, not with a lover's eye, but that of a cuckoo who has laid its egg in a swan's nest.

If you are angry with me, as I must assume you are, I shall not gainsay it. I have betrayed my father's friend. I have betrayed you. I cannot ask you to forgive me. I look for nothing but just fury from you.

After writing those words, I tried to sleep, not wanting to add anything to this letter that might be seen as an attempt to redirect your anger or divert your attention.

A dozen times, I committed to tear up the hateful confession, and a dozen times I told myself that I could not — that you deserved to know the whole truth, however hurtful.

Yet sleep eluded me, and I find myself here, before dawn, listening to a nightingale singing, improbably, out in the square.

The song reminds me that past shame, however stinging, may be soothed by love and beauty. The beauty is yours, which inspires me every bit as much as the gorgeous birdsong. And the love must be mine for you, since I cannot ask yours for me, though I know you have already given it, and freely.

I have reread your letter yet again, and if I respond to some of the things that you said, please do not think that I am trying to cover my shame in any way. I only wish to answer your wonderful words.

As to *Young* Grouse's agelessness, I believe him to be not quite threescore years of age. Yet I can confirm that he has always looked as you see him. When I was a very young boy, when his father was still keeping the grounds, I had very much the same thought that you did: that it should be impossible for someone so old as he to be a son. When I said as much to that estimable man, he winked and told me, "All o'us be *sons*, son. E'en the eldest was a mother's son once upon a time. Don't thee forget that as thee talk with thy elders. They was all boys once."

Mrs. Patchett and Mrs. Reynolds's suggestion of malted barley for Miss Lewis is an excellent one, and one I am sure she and her intended will greatly appreciate.

Concerning my thoughts on marriage, the rights of women, and free love, I think that I shall abstain from commenting at this moment, since I have no reason to believe you will still respect or care for my opinions, which are, in any case, like yours, complex and unclear. Yet permit me to say only that I am the most fortunate of men in my wife, and that is the whole burden of my thoughts on those subjects.

I remember fishing with your uncle, who was a delightful angling companion, and thinking the whole while on the graceful figure and *exquisite eyes* of his niece. I believe that it was your response to meeting me upon the grounds that taught me to hope that your feelings for me might, in fact, be changing — a hope that I must put aside for now.

It seems to me that young Thomas (who will not turn 18 until next spring, when his father will, I believe, grant him the title of Baronet of Badequelle; I have never been asked to call him *Lord Thomas,* though it might be polite, I suppose, to do so) may be interested in your sister. The boy is, as you say, somewhat of a *blank slate.* Given the complications that already exist between our family and his, and given the difference in their stations, and given what I know of his mother, we cannot be certain that his intentions are purely honourable. Yet I have no reason to think them otherwise, not truly. I do not wish Kitty to be hurt, least of all under our care, and so might ask you to keep a closer eye upon the two of them. Were I there, I might ask the young man how he meant to proceed. Until I am there, it might be best to ask Georgiana to play the chaperone. You have suggested that I write her, and I shall, that being one of the thoughts that I shall share with her.

You asked too whether you might be privy to those affairs of business that have stolen me from you. To that my answer is, of course. What is mine is yours, and I should be most happy to share the labour of maintaining our family's fortune with so wonderful a partner. Ask anything and I shall tell you.

Only, do not ask about that last piece of business that your uncle and I are engaged in. I wish it to be a surprise.

The business that we concluded yesterday was the purchase of Jacquard looms for a cotton mill that your uncle has opened in the town of Manchester, Lancashire in which you and I are now partners. Perhaps we may visit there?

I shall sign off now. Junkets is here beside me, far better rested, it seems, than I, and all anxious to take to the road once more. I shall lock your letter with its sisters in my strongbox, and give this to our Cupid.

I have had no dreams of passion, no *signs* of my desire to share with you, alas, since this letter has been largely weighted with other concerns than my love for you.

But trust, I pray you, that that love is undiminished, and this cloud shall pass (like your eclipse), revealing it as bright as the sun.

Regretfully, regrettably, remorsefully,
Yours,

Fitzwilliam Henry, Darcy by birth
(Bennet by God's good Grace)

PS If it will help sail me out of the north of my lady's opinion, then you may call me *Young Willy*. But I beg of you, only in our bed chamber, and only in private. — FHD(B)

Aside – Two Perfect Beauties

From Fitzwilliam Darcy to Georgiana Darcy

Nr 12, Berkeley Sqr
London
August 23

My Dear Sister,

Greetings from London. I hope that the beauties of the summer continue at Pemberley, for here it is as hot and humid as the tropics, but instead of "the spiced Indian air," we are met each morning with the scents of soot and decay. (Lest I make the city seem too unappealing, I will tell you that as I sit here writing you, a nightingale is serenading the square. Its song stills my troubled mind.)

My wife tells me that, in addition to her sister Miss Catherine, you have been enjoying the company of our good friend Miss Giniver, which pleases me enormously. You know that I believe Augustina to be an intelligent, caring young woman, and I have always been pleased to see your friendship grow. And Kitty is quite as delightful as her eldest sister but one, if not quite so serious-minded — and I hope you and even she will forgive me if I say that, while she is very pretty, she is not quite the equal in beauty to my Elizabeth. Then again, I know that both of you will understand when I say that I do not believe that Elizabeth's equal in beauty exists. To my eye, at least, she is the abstract for all beauty, and so any variation, however pleasing, must ultimately be found wanting — aside from your own, of course, which is *sans pareil*. I must think on how it is that there can be two perfect beauties in the world, and both of them living at Pemberley. I am the luckiest of men for many reasons, and while the aesthetic perfection of my wife and sister are not at the pinnacle of those reasons for my felicity, yet your comeliness cannot but help but fill me with pleasure and reflected pride, and so too Elizabeth's.

Speaking of my bride, your new sister — I hope that you have been taking care of her, as I know she has been attempting to take care of you and Kitty. I know that Elizabeth gives an air of self-reliance and accomplishment, yet her letters betray to me that she is, at the very least, lonely, a pain whose cause I can only lay at my own feet, having abandoned her this fortnight. Please, do your best to include her where you can. Let Kitty know that I asked. She may tease Elizabeth that I have asked so — but I believe that Elizabeth will feel better for Kitty's teasing than without it.

My wife tells me that you have lately been reading something in French, and says that she would very much like to join you, her sister, and Miss Giniver (as well as Miss Godwin, who is, Elizabeth tells me, *quite interesting*) — but is held back by her lack of facility with the language, the first fault in her character I have yet detected. Might you find some way to include her in your reading? I know that Elizabeth would be most grateful, and so should I.

My wife also tells me that her sister has taken to using the pet name "Gigi" with you — and that you do not seem to mind. If the name truly pleases you, then it pleases me. If, however, it is merely your natural diffidence that encourages the playful familiarity, and you would rather she stop, please, feel free to let my wife know, and she will find a way to encourage her sister not too presume on your good nature. I know that you are happy to be among friends, and I am happy for you, since you have had too few people of your own age with whom to spend your time and to play. You have occasionally taken me to task for my "unnatural gravity" — I am glad for the opportunity for you to avoid falling into the same trap from which only marriage seems to have saved me.

I will ask you please to keep a watchful eye upon young Master

Giniver. We have discussed, you and I, our uncertain thoughts about the next Lord Malkin's immaturity and about his unsettled nature. Elizabeth tells me that he seems to have taken an interest in her sister, and while I have no objection to their forming a friendship, I do not think the young lord's character well enough formed to trust him blindly with our sister-in-law's honour. Please make sure that Kitty does not find herself in any compromising situations with Master Giniver. You will no doubt think my concerns overblown, but I know that you will indulge me. Should anything untoward happen to Miss Catherine, it would be most dreadful for her, as for her family — and *we* are now her family.

In a similar vein, if you and Miss Catherine could aid Elizabeth in managing the attentions of Lady Malkin, I should appreciate it enormously. Augustina and Thomas's mother is a past-mistress at tea-time jousts at *repartée* and parlor-room verbal fencing, and while I know that Elizabeth has few equals when it comes to wit and spirit, I know too that Lady Malkin has a great deal of experience in administering small, stinging injuries, especially when she is able to single her target out from the herd. Please, see if you and Kitty can do your best not to leave Elizabeth Darcy too much alone with Elizabeth Giniver. I say this as much for Lady Malkin's good as for Mrs. Darcy's, since I know from experience just how capable Elizabeth is of defending herself when roused. I would not come home to find the fields between Pemberley and Langley Park become a pitched battle ground.

I miss you all, my dear Georgiana. I always miss Pemberley when I am away, you know this, but leaving you and Elizabeth behind, it feels as if I have lost the better half of myself.

I shall send this along with the courier later this morning. Do you send your reply by him as well — I long to hear from you.

Your loving brother,

Fitzwilliam Darcy

PS Our doughty courier, John, seems quite taken with you, as I believe
   he should be, since you are beautiful, accomplished, and well-spoken.
   Yet I trust that you recognise that you should not encourage too great

a familiarity with a boy, however entertaining he may be, of circumstances so unequal to your own. I am not encouraging you to cut him out — emphatically not, since I myself like the boy. I am simply encouraging you to avoid leading him on. I do not doubt that you are already acting with all appropriate politeness, and I am simply being a meddling brother. If this is the case, I beg you to forgive me, and wish you, as always, all my love. — FD

11 – Deeper into the Woods

From Elizabeth Darcy to Fitzwilliam Darcy

Pemberley, Derbyshire, *August 23/24*

My dearest ~~Darcy~~ Father Goose,

I am *livid*.

I have been in a foul mood all day, for no reason that I can credit (aside from my *monthly visitor*), and have learned something just now that has tipped my ill humor to full, righteous rage.

And you will never guess who was the instigator and target of that rage.

Go on and guess.

Why yes, my clever husband, it was my bosom friend Elizabeth Giniver, Lady Malkin. How insightful of you to guess!

No, she has not written.

No, she has not come to visit.

Yet even so, she has managed to make an idyllic day at Pemberley (perfect but for your absence) into a scene from a play — from a particularly dreary melodrama, I should say.

In order to tell you how my good friend has managed to enrage me without showing her face, I must begin by telling you about what happened yesterday with my maid Florry after our Cocky Cockney Cupid winged south with my letter for you.

Florry was weeping on the carpet, a figure of abject misery out of one of those self-same melodramas, an affect most unlike her. After Junkets left us, Georgiana, Kitty, and I attempted to calm her, but at first our attentions only seemed to trouble her the more. In particular, Kitty's concern seemed to make Florry quite upset.

At last, I sat her beside me on the sofa by the fire. Georgiana, bless her, served out some tea. Florry sniffled, saying she should not be waited upon by us, but we shushed her and got her to drink some tea.

When at last she had calmed somewhat — tears replaced by the occasional hiccough — I asked her, in as kindly a manner as I could, what had so disturbed her.

This set off a round of self-recrimination on her part, apologizing for having troubled me with her problems, but I assured her that, since I am her mistress, her problems *are* my problems, that I know her to be a sensible girl, and so I trust that whatever had so distressed her must be something of consequence, and that if she could trust me with the cause, I should do all in my power to alleviate it.

The look she gave me then was so admiring, so trusting, I will tell you, Darcy, I almost felt a fraud. Yet having promised to help I waited until she was ready to reveal all.

After much chewing of her lip and worrying of the silk handkerchief that Kitty had given her to wipe her eyes, she at last admitted that she feared that she had got herself "in trouble."

Kitty swooped in, bearing a fresh handkerchief (snatched from my purse), and assured her, breathlessly, that we would help Florry with whatever *trouble* she had got herself in. (Whatever her faults, never let it be said that my youngest sister but one lacks generosity.)

This brought another bout of tears from Florry, and now Georgiana too was assuring her that we would do anything to help Florry.

Having some idea of what sort of *trouble* Florry might be in, I considered, briefly, asking our sisters to leave — to give my maid and me some privacy. And yet they were both being so solicitous, and Florry seemed so distraught — and indeed, it seemed to me that both our sisters are certainly old enough to understand the consequences of certain kinds of *trouble*, especially if they are old enough to be reading the kinds of French novels that make them blush — and so I chose not to send them off. I hope that I did not presume too much. If I did, dear husband, please forgive me. I intended well.

"Florry," I said, "do you fear that you are with child?"

She opened her eyes wide, her lip trembling, and nodded, and then dissolved once more into tears.

Both of our sisters seemed somewhat shocked by the admission, and yet not so surprised as I might have imagined. Kitty frowned. Georgiana's countenance was sad and grave, but still softened by compassion. She took my maid's hand in her own. "Florry," she said, once the girl's tears had subsided once more, "who is the man?"

Now Florry's gaze shot, miserable, to Kitty, who was astonished. "Why do you look at me?"

"Because," whispered Florry, now looking down, "it was Master Thomas."

When we all three expressed surprise, she told us that she had been meeting him in the fields and the woods for some months, that it was "nowt but a bit of fun," that she never expected anything from him, nor had he promised anything, that she knew better than to go *too far*, but they had got carried away — and that now he had only eyes for Miss Kitty, and she was all alone, and her parents would kill her, and I would let her go, and she would be ruined.

It seemed to me that, were her parents to kill her, I should hardly have the opportunity to let her go — a path I did not think I should wish to follow in any case. I assured her that I would not abandon her, that we would find some place for her. I am not sure where in the house a girl whose virtue had been so sullied would be welcome — I was considering how best to approach Mrs. Reynolds — when Georgiana whispered to Florry, "Could your grandmother help, Florry?"

At first I was confused. Then I remembered that Florry's grandmother was in fact Mrs. Grouse. Still, I was uncertain how the midwife could help so early on, as was Kitty.

Your diffident, quiet sister squared her shoulders (though her eyes sought out the floor) and said, "The women of the neighborhood all know that Nanny Grouse is the finest midwife and tender of women's complaints. They also know that they can go to her when they are... in *trouble*."

Kitty's mouth and eyes became perfect circles, as did mine I believe, as we understood what Georgiana was telling us.

And here I must ask that you read on, not as the Honourable Justice of the Peace for the County, but as my beloved husband and your sister's loving brother.

It will not, perhaps, be unknown to you that, in most every town and village, there is some woman who tends to the local wives and daughters, as we have ailments that men — including male doctors — do not suffer nor do not consider worthy of healing. Some are ignorant hedge-witches. Some are little better than quack-salvers who prey upon the desperation and superstition of their charges. But many are women wise in the old ways who provide much needed care to the female sex.

When I was first coming to my womanhood, I was troubled with terrible pains at the onset of my courses, my *monthly visitor*, which, I must own, was scarcely regular enough at the time to be called *monthly*. At my mother's insistence, Mrs. Hill invited a lady who lived outside of Meryton known to all as Mother Bradbury. She came and prescribed a tea of a kind of mint called *pennyroyal* to help with my pains and to make my *visitor* come more regularly. Then she abjured me to be careful not to take such a tea once I should marry, "for ye'll ne'er carry child while ye drink that." Then she winked at Mrs. Hill and said, "Which ye may think a good thing, and all."

All of which is to say that there are ways known to help women who find themselves unexpectedly with child to *solve the problem*, should they choose to do so. If you should care to discuss the morality of such a choice, I should be most willing.

I will say only this much: it seems blatantly unjust that women, who are already less able to defend themselves, must also bear alone the full consequences of *carnal embrace, sexual intercourse, making the beast with two backs,* et cetaera, whether they were willing participants in the act or no. Men can enjoy all of the pleasure (and pleasure you have taught me that it is indeed), while women must pay the price.

The tea, in fact, was very efficacious. I have not had to take it for some years, and I promise you that I have not brought any pennyroyal with me to Derbyshire. When I conceive — when *we* conceive — it shall be the farthest thing possible from *a problem*.

And yet clearly such was not the case for young Florry.

My maid, eyes wide, groaned, "Oh, Nanny'll *kill* us." But she granted that Georgiana was correct, that Mrs. Grouse was the person who might best assist her. And then she grabbed my hand with that not already holding Georgiana's. "Please, Mistress. Please come with us."

And so it was that we all four found ourselves walking out into the Pemberley woods toward the home of the most ancient and renowned house of Grouse.

As Florry led the way, our sisters continued to hold her hands, lending her support. I walked behind, and considered how different this walk in the woods felt from that, just two days before, with Lady Malkin.

We passed the spot where we had encountered Mother Grouse, and I was pleased to see that a heap of earth covered the deadly mushrooms. When we came to the fork where Lady Malkin and I had turned toward the trout creek, however, we took instead the left-hand path, deeper into the woods, a part of the grounds that I am certain I had never visited. We encountered no one — though I thought I spied the figure of a pale woman in servant's garb deep in the shadows, yet when I looked more closely, there was nothing there. A will'o'wisp, perhaps, or my fancy getting the better of me?

The woods grew closer and closer, and the sounds of the forest quieter and quieter, until of a sudden we came into a clearing, and beheld the most extraordinary house that I have ever seen. It looked as if it had *grown* from the ground rather than been built, the stone walls and thick thatch roof seeming somehow far older than the great oaks, elms, and plane trees that surrounded it.

I know that you will have seen the house, and am sure that you will think me fanciful, and yet I could not but think as we approached the entrance that we were about to step into some barrow or fairy fort out of one of the old tales.

On the top of one of the hills near Longbourn, there's an ancient circle of submerged stone — almost an artificial hill itself. We used to climb up to it on a fine day to see the countryside. The stones were carved faintly with whorls and knots much worn with time and weather. We were never able to find an entrance into the barrow, though we looked every time we visited.

Our father liked to tell us that it was an ancient fort, the place where the Romans had defeated Boudicea, Queen of the Britons. Mr. Hill, however, said that it was a fairy place — that there *was* a door into the hill, but it only appeared on certain nights to certain people, and if you were to find such an entrance and go in, you would encounter a beautiful, unearthly palace, much bigger on the inside than the outside, with the tables set for a lavish feast — but that you should never eat the food, no matter how delicious it seemed and how hungry you felt, nor should you go to sleep upon the delightful beds, for if you did either of these, you would never be able to leave the place.

And if you withstood temptation, you might be given the boon of treasure or of a wish, or you might wander the endless stone halls and never find the way out, but if you did, it might be hundreds of years later, though you had only spent a single night in the fairy hill, and everyone you knew would be dead and gone.

Again, I know you will think me fanciful, that it was just a ghost story told to delight and frighten children, yet as Florry brought us into that stone edifice, I did in fact feel as if we were entering another realm, another time.

Inside, the house was shockingly clean and orderly, the hard dirt floor well-swept, the low ceiling hung with a cornucopia of herbs and fruits, most of which I could not begin to identify.

And over by the fire at the far end of the great room, tending a bubbling cauldron like one of Macbeth's Weird Sisters (though it smelled more of mutton stew than eye of newt), stood Mrs. Grouse, as straight-backed as ever, her long, white hair down about her shoulders. She turned her green eyes upon us. "Ay'up, young Florry," she said, hardly seeming surprised to see us. "Who's thee brought t'visit us? Mistress Darcy, ha'th-ee. Miss Georgie, th'art looking right big and proper." She peered at my sister.

I was about to make the introduction, when Kitty burbled, bouncing upon her toes, "I'm Kitty, that is Catherine Bennet, I'm Lizzy — that is, Elizabeth — that is, Mrs. Darcy's sister. It's a pleasure to meet you, Mother Grouse."

"Ay'up," said Mrs. Grouse, smiling wryly, though her eyes were yet shrewd and calculating, flicking from face to face. "And what brings'ee t'our humble cot? Art'ee in need o'our services after all, Mistress *Lizzy* Darcy?"

"Not yet, Mrs. Grouse, thank you. Alas, my husband is away on business, and while I hope to need your *services* most soon, circumstances have not changed at all since last we met." When she nodded, I put my hand upon Florry's shoulder, who jumped at the touch. "We have come with my maid, your granddaughter, who requires your... help."

"Oh, aye?" Mrs. Grouse now peered at Florry, who seemed to shrink under the glare. "And what sort o' help will our Florry be needin'?"

And like a chastened schoolboy, Florry poured forth the whole of the tale in a single torrent, just as she'd told it to us.

Mrs. Grouse stood and listened, unblinking, face like granite. When Florry finally finished, trickling to a dribble of an end rather than a full stop, her grandmother tutted, "Silly girl. Ha' we not taught'ee better?"

And then she began to poke and prod Florry, much to the girl's evident embarrassment. She pulled down Florry's lids and peered into her eyes, yanked down her chin and peered down her throat. Tutting again and shaking her head, Mrs. Grouse turned Florry about and began to unbutton her dress — though my maid looked alarmed, neither she nor any of us felt able to object.

Mrs. Grouse then proceeded to poke and prod once more, now beneath my maid's cloths, leaving poor Florry looking thoroughly discomfited.

The grandmother's expression, though still grave, became more and more perplexed, until at last she went down on her knees and under Florry's skirts. Still frozen, Florry released a squawk of distress at whatever Mrs. Grouse was doing, but it did not last long.

Mrs. Grouse released a string of barely intelligible invective and came back out from beneath Florry's dress. Standing straight as an arrow, her arms crossed, her expression now plainly disgusted, she snarled, "Art'ee carryin' t'Second Comin', girl? Did t'Holy Spirit come an' visit'ee and get'ee wi'child?"

"No, Nanny!" spluttered Florry.

"Girl, us's had many a girl younger'n thee come to us and ask us for *help* when they's *in trouble*," Mrs. Grouse growled, and spat upon the dirt floor. "*But ne'er a girl who's still a virgin!*" When Florry shrank before the onslaught, Mrs. Grouse continued, "Did our Annie raise a simpleton? Did'ee no' listen when us and thy mother talked t'thee? Does'ee no' know how *babes are made*? Must us tell'ee once't'gain 'bout t'bulls'n't'cows? Tell us how'ee thinks thee be *pregnant* when there's ne'er been any pizzle in thy cunny!"

Trembling, face bright red, Florry began to try to straighten her dress. I went to do up the buttons in the back, happy, under the circumstance, to play my maid's maid.

As I did, Florry poured forth a further, clearer tale of the "bit of fun" that she had engaged in with Master Giniver when they had gone "too far." Apparently, just before our wedding, they had been enjoying each other's company in the wheat fields on the eastern edge of our estate — a place where they might *play* without being discovered, given the height of the grain this late in the season — when they had both found themselves naked. "We was doin' nowt but kissin' and ticklin'!" swore Florry, blushing so violently that I feared she might faint at any moment. But the *tickling* had led to *our Tommy* having a *go*, an eruption, the contents of which had covered what Florry somewhat delicately referred to as her *belly*.

"And then," wept my maid, "*us haven't had our monthlies since, and it's been weeks and weeks!*"

At last, Mrs. Grouse's thunderous expression softened. "Silly girl," she grunted, but took her granddaughter in her arms. Over Florry's quaking shoulder, the midwife peered at me, her look still calculating, but for the first time with some warmth. "Tell us, young Florry. After thy *bit o' fun* wi' young Master Tommy, did owt else change for thee?"

Florry granted that, a few days later, she had become my lady's maid.

"Oh, aye?" said Mrs. Grouse. "And has'ee spent much time wi' thy new mistress, girl?"

"'Course, Nanny." Though Florry was facing away from me, I could yet see her posture twist as she considered this. "All day, every day."

"And when thee's no' wi' thy mistress, thee's handlin' her clothes?"

Florry nodded, still sniffling.

"Girl, pu' two healthy young women such as thee and Mistress Lizzy together all day and nigh', and they'll change the time o' they's courses, sure 'nough." She waved a rigid finger between her granddaughter's back and me. "'Tis t'smell, aye?"

"Oh," said Florry, Kitty, Georgiana, and I.

Soon thereafter, we took our leave of Mrs. Grouse. I thanked her for her help and offered to pay for her time.

The old woman actually laughed, and waved away my offer. "Florry's our own. Her care is our responsibility, no' thine. Mind, such a mutton-head, she might no' be one o' ours, after t'all." When Florry's face fell, her grandmother laughed again and embraced her once more, kissing her upon both cheeks.

Then we left, our journey back to Pemberley a much lighter one than the journey out.

Though I was not of a mind to tease my maid, Florry was in an understandably giddy mood, and soon we were all laughing about her comedy of errors — greatly relieved that it had turned out a comedy after all, though none of us said so much. Even Georgiana took part in the laughter, which was a pleasure to see. I have come to realise that Florry and Georgiana, being of an age, were almost certainly friends before I came to Pemberley, and I feel that I have disrupted their friendship — most selfish of me.

I was thinking, I will be honest, that I now understood perhaps why my own *monthlies* should be late, when Mrs. Grouse was certain I was not with child. The explanation was less exhilarating than the one that I had been nurturing — that you and I had conceived, Mrs. Grouse's assurances notwithstanding — but also a great deal less terrifying.

When the fog of these preoccupations cleared, I realised that Kitty was peppering Florry with a fusillade of questions about Thomas, some of which would have crossed the border of propriety and made a full-on invasion of the modest lands beyond, had we not all just heard the tale of their naked tryst in the corn.

Warming to her theme, all pretense of her own reserve abandoned, Florry told Kitty that, in spite of his seemingly bland affect, Tommy could be quite playful and funny, "for a toff." She continued that he was very young for his age, that between his parents and his sister, he hadn't developed any great social skill, "but he's a nice enough lad under all, even so."

Kitty seemed delighted with this answer, though I could tell that Georgiana was as dubious as I. I attempted to engage your sister, but she shrugged off my attempt at conversation, and so I let it go for the moment.

Soon, we were out of the woods and into the sunshine, and Pemberley rose before us.

Florry stopped and turned to me, face prim and eyes downcast. "Mistress Darcy," she said, "Us... I promise that I won't ever do owt so silly, Mistress. I's had the scare of me life, and having Nanny poking about at me — I would understand if you were to think me unsuited to your service after such a mess as this." When I told her that of course I would keep her on, that she had been an excellent lady's maid, and nothing that I had seen that day changed that fact, she looked relieved, and then peered at me, at Kitty, and at Georgiana. "May I then ask you all, ladies, to say nowt about this to anyone at the house? I am honoured that you all are so understanding of my *mistake*, but I do not think..." She trailed off and looked down again.

Kitty and Georgiana both embraced the girl, as would I had they not beaten me to it, and we all solemnly promised her that we would say nothing of that day's events to anyone at the house — or outside.

However, I told her, "I shall have to inform Mr. Darcy. I know you are very aware of his discretion and his honourable nature — I cannot think that he will in any way think worse of you for such a relatively innocent and inconsequential mistake. Yet he deserves to know." And so he now does.

You will be pleased to know that she blanched at this, but granted that it was only just.

And then the girls all began to tease me about our letters to each other, and about our tireless Cupid — Kitty to start with, but Florry and even Georgiana soon enough — and we were all laughing as we came back into Pemberley, just in time for supper.

Last night, my courses came, and I wept — in small part for the tenderness that even now accompanies them (though not as extreme as the pains I suffered when first they visited me), and in small part for the loss of the faint hope that we had already sparked life between us, in spite of what Mrs. Grouse had told me.

Though little moved to amorous thoughts in my discomfort, I yet found myself dreaming, as I drifted off to sleep, of you atop me and within me, once more filling me with your love, once more working with me to *conceive* in a way that neither of us can yet fully conceive, though I, like you, look forward to assaying and, in the end, to comprehending completely and utterly.

This morning, as she opened the drapes, Florry informed me that she too had begun her *monthlies*, though she was far more unadulterated in her delight, the cramps notwithstanding.

At breakfast, I had a very circumspect, but I hope very clear conversation with our sisters (but particularly Kitty) about Augustina's brother. Though they both clearly understood me, I made Kitty promise that she would go nowhere with Master Giniver without, at the very least, his sister, myself, or Georgiana. She assured me that she would do so. Then she added that she needed, in any case, to give the young heir *a piece of her mind*. When I tried to dissuade her — not wanting to worsen Florry's embarrassment — Kitty gave me a look she has only given me perhaps a half a dozen times in all her life: a look that assured me that she was not playing, and that she would do what she had said she was going to do.

I abandoned my argument, but promised myself not to leave them alone if I could help it.

Some time before mid-day, three figures came striding up the drive to the house — one dark-haired, and two bright, sunset red, and I was pleased to see them — though I was now most curious and cautious about Master Giniver, given all that we had learned about him yesterday.

Nevertheless, Kitty and Georgiana were as delighted to welcome them as I, and we had Mrs. Patchett arrange a kind of *picnic* on the veranda overlooking the lake and the beautiful scene beyond, which was in all its glory.

As we ate, I asked Miss Godwin why she had come when Mr. Shelley had stayed at Langley Park.

She informed me that he and Mr. Lackey were busy *entertaining* Lady Malkin, and that she felt as if there might be better sport to be had elsewhere. She said this very lightly, glancing at Augustina, who was laughing with our sisters and her brother, but I could not help but sense some bitterness beneath her air of disinterest.

I am discovering that, every day, I find new reasons to dislike Lady Malkin — although one must admire her commitment to her chosen field of study, as well as her endurance.

Once we had finished the excellent luncheon, and the servants had cleared away the food and plates, I was about to suggest we all go for a walk, when Kitty rounded on Thomas. "What is this that I hear about you, Master Giniver?" she said, as imperiously as her slight frame could allow. "That you have been leading young girls astray in the fields?"

In young Tommy's defense, he looked quite abashed at Kitty's accusation. He attempted to defend himself, but could scarcely get more than a half a dozen words out than he wilted beneath her glare, which I must grant was worthy of our mother — or perhaps even your aunt, Lady Catherine. It was not quite as impressive as Mrs. Grouse's, but it certainly threw him from his guard.

"Oh, Tommy," sighed Augustina, "have you been playing at silly buggers with the servants again?"

"Again?" asked Kitty, her fury even more impressive.

"It… It wasn't one of *our* servants!" When he saw that neither Augustina nor any of the others were at all impressed by this argument, least of all Kitty, who now seemed to be towering before him, he got on his knees and tried to plead. "It was only the one!" said Thomas, voice choked. He glanced at me, and I knew that he was aware that the young woman with whom he had been disporting himself was now my maid. "And… and *she* wanted to…. And… and I… and nothing *happened!*"

"Oh," said Kitty, "nothing happened to *you,* Tommy, but the young girl thought you might have got her in a *family way.*"

Thomas's face turned pale as curdled milk. "But… but… We *didn't…!*"

"Excuse me, Lizzy," said Kitty. "I should like to continue this discussion with Tommy just over in the garden." When I raised a silent eyebrow, she responded with her most meek and compliant expression, apparently to let me know that she would not leave our sight. It is an expression that might have reassured me had I not seen it previously on Kitty's face on occasions when she and Lydia had gone on to some of their most noted occasions of mischief. Nonetheless, I nodded in accession and she led Tommy down among the roses my mother so admired — far enough that they could speak with each other in some privacy, but close enough that we could still see them.

Georgiana seemed to be informing Thomas's sister and Miss Godwin of the events earlier in the day, though without revealing the identity of the servant whose honour young Master Giniver had (so very nearly) sullied. Mary appeared to be listening with quiet fascination, while Augustina seemed by turns appalled and amused. "Look at Tommy," she laughed, and indicated where my tiny sister was berating her tall brother, who twitched in mortified silence. "He looks like one of Signor Galvani's frogs."

"Galvani?" asked Georgiana, while Mary returned her dark gaze to Augustina, who nodded, her copper curls bouncing. She proceeded to launch into a breathless discussion of *Leyden jars* (which are, apparently, devices for storing lightning — or *electrical ether)* and *spasmodic muscular contractions.* I was largely lost — and somewhat repelled — by the rehearsal, but Georgiana and Mary seemed quite taken by the discussion. They began to ask searching questions of a nature that seemed, to this uneducated country wife, to be far from the topic of twitching frog's legs, yet which seemed to take up all of their attention, so that when my sister led Mr. Giniver (who was still white-faced, but no longer twitching) back from the garden, they scarcely noticed.

"Lizzy," said Kitty, "Mr. Giniver has something to say to a member of your staff." When she looked at him, still imperious, he nodded gravely.

I stood and whispered, "I shall come with you, if you do not mind." I then told the three young natural philosophers that we would be back soon. Georgiana nodded in acknowledgement. The other two scarcely paused in their colloquy.

Then I led Tommy and Kitty up to our bed chamber, where I knew that Florry would be working. When I opened the door, she turned to give me her customary merry greeting, but gaped as Kitty and Tommy followed me into the room and dipped into a hurried curtsy.

I was just about to affect an introduction when it struck me how absurd it would be for me to do so. As I attempted to think of a way to fill the awkward silence, Kitty stepped forward, still in her imperious mode, and said, "Miss Gwynn, Master Giniver has something he wishes to say to you."

Florry now looked quite frozen with astonishment, her eyes, usually wry and lively, flown wide in shock.

Tommy looked at Florry, his fair face turning red, then white, then red again. When he looked back to my sister, she simply raised an eyebrow. He swallowed hard, and turned back to my maid. "Florry," he began, before stammering once more to a halt. "Miss Gwynn. I apologise most heartily for having taken advantage of the difference in our stations and so compromised your honour." Having once opened his mouth, Tommy then poured forth an expression of such profound and apparently sincere regret that Florry and I could do nothing but stand and listen, like generals overseeing an unending parade of soldiers. Florry attempted to stem the flood — no doubt to tell Tommy that she had been, at the least, an equal participant in their sport (for so she had assured us), but Tommy would not or could not stop, once started, and so we contented ourselves to riding the torrent to its conclusion. Kitty, in the meanwhile, listened to Master Giniver's abject self-abasement with an air of maidenly victory.

As Tommy continued, I considered just how it was that my sister might believe herself to be benefitting from the whole embarrassing affair. My thought was this: flirt though she may be, my sister is not altogether a fool. Master Thomas Giniver, the future Earl Malkin, has shown her attentions that I am quite certain she knows must skirt the limits of social propriety, given the distances between her station and his. I believe that, by encouraging Tommy to abase himself so thoroughly before her, she wishes to place herself — in his mind, at least — not as his inferior, nor as his equal, but as his *better*. If so, she is playing a game of social status with which I am not altogether comfortable. I am, as you know, an egalitarian at heart (though by no means a Revolutionary). I understand, even so, the realities of station, class, and rank, being the daughter of a poor country gentleman, yet I have always chosen to treat everyone with the same respect — or, if your aunt Catherine is to be believed, with even-handed *dis*respect. Kitty, it seems, may see rank as a game — a ladder to climb. If so, I must speak to her about it, since I am not sure that it is a game that she can win, and, losing, one whose cost I doubt that she can afford to bear.

Once Tommy had finally stumbled to the end of his apology, he glanced to Kitty, who nodded, and then, expectantly, to my maid.

Eyes still wide, Florry looked to me. I could only demur, and so she turned to face the young man. "Tom — My lord. You honour me by condescending to offer so fulsome an apology to so humble a servant." (I will swear upon all that I hold dear — beginning with your gracious self — those are the very words she spoke. I believe my maid has a greater facility with tongues than her mistress!) She continued, "As it has all come to nowt, er, *naught*, and since you were at no greater fault in what might have happened than… than I, perhaps it is best if we were to close the book and *get on with us*, as me nanny would say."

Then the two former co-frolickers blinked and looked first to their mistresses and then back to each other. Tommy gave a deep, stiff bow from the waist while Florry delivered a floor-brushing curtsy worthy of court, and my sister led Master Giniver back out of our bedchamber. Not wanting to leave the two alone — more worried, if I am honest, about Tommy than Kitty — I told the still-shocked Florry that she had done well, and raced to join the lost lambs.

When we returned to the veranda, Augustina was continuing to hold forth about *electrical ether,* much to the fascination of Georgiana and Miss Godwin. (I too was fascinated, but had, I will admit, some difficulty following the details of their discussion.) She began to describe how a galvanic flow might, some day, be used for carrying messages from one side of the country to the other "in the blink of an eye," and I could only think how wonderful that would be — to write to you and have my words brought to you on instant bolts of lightning, rather than the determined gallop of an erstwhile poet from Moorgate.

Ever-sensible Georgiana asked, "But since the ether is invisible, how would one read such a message?" and we all of granted that it was a good question, even Augustina, who said that much needed to be done, but that in our lifetimes, the post would become a thing of the past.

And I realised then that while I should dearly love to be able to communicate with you without delay, I should miss the sight of the ink you had laid, the feel of the paper, and, of course, the smell of your *essence,* your *passion*. (I have got out your letter to smell the distinctive perfume of your seed more than once a day since it arrived, dear husband, and it has brought an answering passion from me every time, even as uncomfortable as I currently am.) Unless these electrical letters of the future can communicate all the senses, then I think they will be poor substitutes indeed.

Odd Mary was listening to the whole of the conversation with her eyes closed, humming to herself. Of a sudden, the lids flew open and she asked, like some sibyl of old, "But could this ether bring life?"

When we all expressed astonishment at the question, she went on to point out that it could make muscle in dead frogs move, that perhaps it was itself the "essence of life" — that perhaps the spark that makes us think and move and breathe and love is nothing more or less than a co-alescence of this energy.

This evoked much conversation and laughter, as I am sure you will understand. We began to discuss, if each of us might create *life,* what should it look like?

I, alone of the party, thought that, perhaps, it might not be such a good idea. From whence morality or intelligence? Could a creature creat-ed by one of us ever surpass its master in those gifts that makes a human creature more than an animal?

This naturally gave life to a passionate and most interesting discus-sion. Even Kitty and Tommy, who mostly seemed to be interested in each other, shared their thoughts, but the conversation was largely among Miss Giniver, Miss Godwin, and of course Miss Darcy, all of whom seemed quite animated on the subject (if I may use the word).

At one point they turned to the question of whether *love* were a nec-essary component for creating *life.* And if not, what *was* love?

While they debated *that* momentous subject, I found myself think-ing that, indeed, I should after all like to create life — with you. I look forward to attempting to do so as soon as you return. I may not be able to wait for you to enter the house, and so I will make sure that the wheat in the eastern fields remains unharvested.

Soon, the sun crept behind the house, and the Langley Park party were forced to say goodbye, promising to return the next day. (Miss Godwin said that she might be otherwise engaged on the morrow — today — but that she would see if she could get Percy to join them.) Tommy made a great point of leading Kitty out of earshot — though not out of sight — to take his leave, so that we saw him bow to *kiss her hands.*

I am delighted for my sister that he, usually so restrained of aspect (in public, at least), shows her such passionate devotion. I must admit, however, I am not completely at ease with their continued courtship. For Master Giniver, I now believe that he is not so vicious or rakish as he is young and, oddly, innocent. I do not believe that he intended any ill to Florry, nor any particular disrespect — I believe that he was led by a desire for pleasure, which, while not admirable, is certainly an understandable and most common failing. And Kitty seems to be attempting to train him at least to attempt to stay within the bounds of propriety, if only for the reward of her favour.

But what might his parents think of such a match? Lady Malkin would, I am certain, be appalled, and Lord Malkin, whom I do not know except by her less than flattering reports, cannot be pleased, I fear.

But perhaps I get ahead of myself. They are both young, in spirit and in years. This may all be but a game — the entertainment of a summer and naught else.

Speaking of games, I asked Kitty at supper whether she remembered the rules of Tom-o'-Straw. She got very quiet and serious as she considered this question — for Kitty takes play *very* seriously, as you know. When she answered, her response restored only a little to my plundered store of memory: the game was played around a scarecrow, as I remembered, with one person starting the game as *Tom,* the straw man's *keeper* or *jailor.* Each of the other players attempted to get a piece of straw from the figure, but then *Tom* would attempt to touch or (as was often the case) to tackle them before they could get away. Those who had been touched (or tackled) became Tom's helpers, the *bailies,* and aided in guarding the scarecrow. The game ended when each of the free players held a piece of straw or had been captured.

This all fit with my memory — but Kitty went on to say that there were many more rules that she could scarce remember, to do with when one had and hadn't been captured, and whether one could *rescue* Tom's helpers, and if one could use the tall corn as a hiding place (which made me think of Florry and Tommy), and so on. (The game was, now that I think on it, largely played after the harvest, since most of us were the children of farmers and knew the wrath that trampled fields would bring down on us.) Then she gave a characteristically playful giggle and said, "Mostly, I believe the game was an excuse for the boys and girls to run about and wrestle." This made Georgiana blush, but it also made her laugh, which I will consider a good thing.

As I prepared for bed, I asked Florry how she felt about Tommy's apology.

She said that she had found the whole ordeal mortifying, but that she supposed that it was a good thing that the lordling learn as memorable a lesson as the lady's maid. Then she laughed, made a rather ribald comment about the rapidity of the young lord's "let-go," wished me a good night, and left me to my sleep, which was sound and filled with dreams searching for you among fields of high grain.

This morning, I conferred with those domestic high priestesses, Mrs. Reynolds and Mrs. Patchett, about Miss Lewis's wedding gift. They said that they have sent two hundredweight of barley to germinate and dry, so, I discovered, to make malt, such as brewers prize; it should be ready to be presented in two or three days.

When I admitted that I wished I had thought to make the presentation at my first visit to the kitchens, both women tutted, assuring me that none of the staff thought the worse of me for it, and certainly, said Mrs. Patchett, not Fanny Lewis, who had seemed pleased with my visit and my little speech — pleased to be remembered by the lady of the house, and pleased to have her coming marriage recognised.

Georgiana and Kitty joined me for a walk through the woods. I once again could have sworn I saw a female figure, all dressed in servants' garb, but when I turned to show our sisters, there was, once again, no one there. Kitty and even Georgiana teased me, saying that I was seeing some apparition, come to haunt me for treating the Pemberley servants so ill. I assured them that they were not in the least amusing, which caused them to tease me all the more.

Their taunting continued through the rest of the walk, and up to our luncheon, which we took once again outside, for the weather was glorious. Also, I believe that Kitty and Georgiana both wished to look out for the Giniver siblings, who arrived with Miss Godwin on foot just as we began our meal of a cold pigeon pie. Pink-faced and freckled, the two red-heads begged to join us — but only if we could remove indoors, since the sun had been fierce on their fair skin. And so we moved to the library, where Mrs. Reynolds met us with a jug of some sort of lemon cordial, which all of us found delightful, most especially Augustina and Tommy.

As we finished our light meal, I once again asked Miss Godwin where Mr. Shelley might be. She informed me that the poet and his friend Mr. Lackey had joined Lord Malkin at hunting in the park and would likely not be seen until the evening. That Lady Malkin was abroad, and the present company more than pleasant, and so she had joined with Augustina and Thomas again in the walk to Pemberley. She hoped she was welcome, which of course we all assured her she was, though I sensed from Master and Miss Giniver that Miss Godwin's company had not precisely been *sought*.

Then again, Miss Giniver, for all her many virtues, frequently seems ill at ease, and Tommy's opinions are difficult to ascertain at the best of times. And so perhaps I was imagining it.

After we had finished our meal — servants appearing like fairy spirits to bear away the leavings — our company talked for a while about nothing and nothing again. After yesterday's philosophical fancies, perhaps we were all happy to remain firmly planted on the ground. Kitty and Mary both complimented Augustina on the cut of her gown, which seemed to catch Miss Giniver by surprise, and she stared down at the dress, as if she had forgot what she were wearing. Georgiana and Tommy talked of the weather.

I began to look for the wonderful volume of Homer that I had been enjoying, but could not find it. A general search was made, to no avail. I think perhaps young Junkets may have secreted it away to the room where he has been sleeping — or where I *hope* that he has been sleeping. I should not put it past the young man to have lain awake reading instead.

During the search, the famous green volume of French prose appeared as if out of thin air, and Augustina began to read from it, much to our sisters' apparent delight. Tommy, however, complained that he could not follow the language, and if they were to read aloud, it ought to be something that everyone present could understand. Augustina and our sisters both apologised and began to suggest English books we might all enjoy, but Mary plucked the French book from Augustina's fingers and offered to translate it.

The other three young women did not look at all comfortable with this plan. Augustina scowled and Kitty's eyes flew from me to Tommy, while Georgiana stared fixedly down at the hem of her gown. Tommy, however, was delighted, and I, of course, was only too happy to discover just what questionable literary delights our sisters had been enjoying, and so we begged Mary to do so.

And so she began reading to us from what revealed itself to be an epistolary novel of the Old Regime with a title that Mary translated as *Perilous Meetings*. The letter that Mary began with was from a Viscount to his possible lover and apparent mentor in intrigue, a Countess (or a *Marquise?*) with whom he was engaging in some sort of conspiracy of revenge to seduce the virtuous wife of a man who had in some way offended the Countess — or possibly the Viscount, or possibly both. As Mary read on, Kitty, Georgiana, and Augustina attempted to set the *dramatis personae* and the scene, but I am afraid that they were not always clear or in agreement in their whispered *marginalia*.

In any case, the Viscount's letter largely involved a story about an acquaintance's simultaneous seduction of three ladies in his Paris villa, of how the acquaintance carried off the trick masterfully, and how each of the ladies believe her lover to be hers alone — until the next day, when all three ladies came down to dine together. At which point, our hero (the Viscount's acquaintance) revealed all, to the women's general consternation.

I will tell you that, compared to *Fanny Hill*, it was far less explicit in describing amorous activities — yet the overall air of moral turpitude was disquieting.

In any case, the Viscount was, it seems, attempting to dissuade the Countess from meeting herself with the acquaintance, lest she become merely another of the man's playthings.

Mary passed the book to Augustina, who translated — rather more precisely, I think, but less artistically — a letter of a very different tone between a young cavalier and his Juliet. In it, the knight promised his lady love that they would overcome the barriers between them — with the aid, it seems, of the Viscount and of the Countess, and so we, as the readers, were clearly to understand that the young lovers were being misled in their pursuit of True Love. The lovers, of course, were completely unaware of this. The shift in tone was remarkable — and I began to see where the attraction in the book might be. A vulgar book about vulgar people can only entertain for so long, even a sparkling-ly witty one, but a book that presents the affairs of a wide variety of people seems much more interesting to me.

It is still, I think, a somewhat vulgar book, but an interesting one.

When the letter ended, Augustina passed the volume to your sister, who seemed determined not to allow her own, becoming modesty to keep her from participating. She began to read us the Countess's response to the letter from the Viscount.

It was a fascinating contrast — Georgiana's quiet, polite voice speak-ing the Countess's vehement, angry response to the Viscount's letter. She excoriated him for daring to tell her what to do — a censure that Mary and Augustina much applauded, though Kitty felt it was undeserved.

And then the Countess began to recount her history by way of show-ing just how little she needed the Viscount's aid, and as Georgiana read on, I had the strange sense of having heard the story before.

As she began to say how she had begun her research into how best to acquire those qualities on which she now prided herself, that feeling grew, and when she recounted the tale of how she had attempted her first seduction — *of her confessor* — by telling him that she had "done all that women do with men," I was filled both with astonishment and with growing rage.

"When was this book written, Georgiana?" I asked, knowing that it must have been printed some decades ago, when my *great friend Betsy Giniver* could have been at best a girl.

Somewhat flustered, Georgiana turned to the front of the book, and informed me that it had been printed in Paris some thirty years ago, some years before what you termed *La Terroir (La Terreur?)*. "Yet it is not *so* old-fashioned a book!" she assured me, concerned at my disapproval.

I assured her that it was not, that I enjoy epistolary novels enor-mously, and that the story was most entertaining, but that something that she had read had struck me, and so I wished to know more about the book's provenance. I thanked her, attempting to calm my growing fury, and begged her to continue.

For it was clear to me: Lady Malkin had, in revealing to me her story and her self, as I thought, stolen at the very least that one passage of a book published before she reached her womanhood. I felt lied to — for since I had not asked for the lady's confidence, the abuse of my trust could not be anything but intentional.

Georgiana read on. And while the contrast between her demure whisper and the Countess's continued full-throated self-justification continued to be entertaining, yet the story continued to follow — line for line, and, in many cases, word for word — the story that Elizabeth Giniver had *confessed* to me two days ago in the woods.

Why?

Why would she do such a thing?

What was her possible aim in misleading me so? Simply to do it, for her own amusement? That seems in character, I suppose, but completely pointless. Did she have some other motive, as yet obscure?

I could not say.

Yet by the time that Georgiana had finished the letter from *Madame la Marquise*, I was overcome with wrath of a kind that only you have ever evoked in me.

Yet I am quite certain that the outcome now shall be quite different, and that this time no prejudice is blinding me.

I begged the pardon of our sisters and the guests, pleading headache (which I had in fact developed), and retreated to our chamber, where I have now been writing to you ever since. I sent poor Florry away, not wishing to snap at her, and have filled some twenty-five sheets of this lovely paper front and back telling you of the past few days and how it came that I am in such a fury.

The sun is low and I fear that I am missing supper — no doubt Florry will return soon with some delicious meal of Mrs. Patchett's concoction — but I cannot stop pouring forth my anger in this letter. I have nothing else to say, nothing else to tell you, and my anger, which had begun to abate, is now as fresh and raw as ever, now that I have recounted its cause.

I have glanced out the window just now and seen the one thing that might have restored my mood: a rider coming up the drive. Alas, it does not seem to be you, oh, woe is me! Yet it does look like our good friend Junkets, and I shall run down to the front hall to meet him now and take your words, which are the only thing that I can count on to lighten my stygian mood.

Oh, Darcy.

Oh, my dearest, dearest Darcy.

You have indeed lightened my mood completely, though you had no intent of doing so.

I have read your earnest confession of your fears at first with growing concern — for nothing, I promise, but your state of mind — and then with wild amusement.

Oh, my sweet, sweet husband!

What kind of husbandman do you call yourself?

Augustina your daughter by Elizabeth Giniver?

My laughter has alarmed the servants, who came, fearing that I was having some sort of fit. I explained that you had sent me a very funny joke in your letter. They took this explanation with equanimity, though I could tell that it did not match their expectation of the sorts of letters that you would write to your wife.

Well, my sweetest, dearest Darcy, I shall completely discount all of your confession as untrue on the face of it.

If you ask me for proof, I shall point you no further than the halls of Pemberley and of Langley Park, and if that does not settle the question for you, then I shall simply laugh at you as I have promised Georgiana that I should do, after all.

I believe that you are very sweet, nonetheless, for taking so to heart your own honour, your father's friend's, and his daughter's. If it were possible for you to rise higher in my esteem, I promise you should do so.

Yet you are a silly boy.

If I am to be Mother Goose, you must clearly be Father Goose, and so I have re-styled you in the salutation.

I am glad to hear your defense of Lord Malkin, for I have heard nothing ill of the man aside from Lady Malkin's slurs. I like his daughter (*his* daughter, without question!), and my sister likes his son, and so I should be horrified to find that *both* of their parents were despicable.

Thank you so much for sharing your news of business with me. I do wish to share the burden with you if I can. I am delighted that we have become partners in business with my uncle Edward, as he has always struck me as a most prudent and conscientious man, and I believe that such a partnership will serve all of our fortunes well.

I should love to visit Lancashire with you. I should love to visit *anywhere* with you. Never leave me ever again, please, dear Darcy! Swear you won't!

(I know that you cannot swear so — that we will be parted again for reasons good and ill. Yet I cannot bear to think of it just now.)

I seem to remember that it was on the road from London to Manchester that my uncle passed through this neighborhood and met my aunt. Perhaps we can all four visit this factory together?

What indeed is a *Jacquard* loom? I have heard the name mentioned in the newspapers, but never any explanation of what it might be — and since we now own several, I should love to know more.

I should love, too, to explore London's many wonders with you. I have visited the city several times, but have gone with my aunt and uncle to only a few performances and none of the exhibitions that one hears of. I can scarcely wait to see them together. And perhaps I shall even tempt you to some balls? I know you dance well, and wish to show you off to all of the other ladies, so that they can see what I have and they cannot.

I am glad that we both felt the same divided gladness and sorrow at Jane and Charles seeing you before we saw each other. I hope that their good humor gives you joy; tell me how you find them.

Likewise, I look forward to joining you in our Berkeley bed. Oh, husband, we have so many places to explore our love, to *fuck,* inside and out! *I have bought the mansion of a love, but not possess'd it!* Or rather, *two* mansions, with many rooms, and that is not mentioning the gardens, the woods, the lake, and of course the wheat fields. We must possess them all!

But I do look forward to losing myself in your embrace, there in our *other* big bed, in our *other* house. Even at noon, how can the nightingale *help* but sing in Berkeley Square while our love finds its fullest expression?

Florry has indeed come up with food, and very sternly made me promise to eat it — and then to go down to reassure our sisters that I am well. I shall lock this letter away and finish it — though I am beginning to feel it shall prove as endless as Penelope's tapestry — after I come back to the room.

I need to find more paper anyway — this was the last sheet in my desk.

I have been *good* Lizzy and eaten my supper, and visited our sisters, who were entertaining young Junkets in the library — or rather, he was entertaining them, reading from the very book of Homer that I had failed to find this afternoon. He had read far past where I had got — he was reading the scene where young Nausicaa and her playmates find naked, shipwrecked Ulysses there on the sands. He was reciting aloud to Kitty and Georgiana with such pleasure in the story and in the language that he was actually weeping as he read.

When he noticed that I had arrived, he stopped, apologizing and standing.

I assured him that he need not move on my account, nor stop in his reading, since he and the young ladies were so clearly enjoying it.

Georgiana pleaded with him to continue, and Kitty added her voice as well.

And so he read on, up through the beginning of the actual tale that I think of as *The Odyssey* — of the departure from Troy and the long journey home. There was something about his Cockney voice reading those gorgeous words — somewhat like the contrast between Georgiana's sweet voice and the Countess's cynicism early today — that was strangely delightful.

At last he paused, and remarked how beautiful the book was.

Georgiana asked whether he had not read the story before.

He assured her that he had, in school, when they were learning Greek, but that his master's translations were dull and stale by comparison. "Reading this," he said, eyes bright, "I feel like an explorer spying some unknown ocean."

Then he apologised — he had *borrowed* the book after his last visit, and it had come with him to London and back. He told us that his thoughts as he rode both to Bloomsbury and to Pemberley had been filled with Homer, that it felt as if his mind were bursting with the poetry.

Then he made to hand the book back to me, but I refused. "I can imagine that volume giving no one more joy than it is giving you, my dear Junkets. You have been doing me and my husband an enormous service. Please, keep the book."

I hope that I have not been too prodigal in my gift — I know that the book is some century or more old, and likely to have stayed in Pemberley's library the whole time.

And yet I could not, in good conscience, *not* give the book to one who would so deeply appreciate it.

He thanked me profusely, and asked if I had my reply to you ready, for he would leave tonight.

I told him that under no circumstances was he to leave without having eaten and slept — I did not want him falling off the horse! — and that I would bring my reply to him in the morning.

Georgiana said that she too would have a letter for him to bring you — by which I understand that you have indeed written her as I suggested. I thank you for indulging me, and I am happy to say that your sister looked much livelier this evening than she did this afternoon — and I believe that is only partly due to our wildly entertaining troubadour.

From Mrs. Reynolds I have obtained a sheaf of paper that would make my father weep for joy at its profligate size and quality. I shall fill every sheet, husband, I promise.

I promise not to ask about your last piece of business, though I am filled with curiosity now, as I am sure you knew I would be. Yet I will show you that I can be patient, even as I beg you to conclude the business speedily, and to come home to me.

With my *surprise* in hand, of course.

Your love is the sun that brightens my soul, all day and all night — in your presence and even in your absence (though I prefer the former). Even during an eclipse the sun is still there — it is only our sight that is obscured. And so I shall dream of the return of the light — and of your gracious person, which I look forward to enjoying as we continue to *possess our mansion*.

With love, and laughter, and ever love, yours,

~~Elizabeth Anne Bennet Darcy~~

Mother Goose, OSG

PS My *visitor* is soon to depart. I look forward to answering your passion with more of my own. — EABD

PPS You could never be further from the *North of my opinion*. I shall call you *Young Willy* only in our bed, and only when unclothed, even as you asked. It shall be my great pleasure to do so. Alas, I cannot promise that I shall not call it out *very loudly*, since you inspire such excesses in me. La, I am sure they shall here me all the way to the old city of York. *Oh, young Willy!* I shall scream. *Fuck me! Fuck my cunt, young Willy! Oh!* — EABD

PPPS This morning, no weeping maid met me as I entered the library — just Georgiana and Junkets. She was handing him a letter, which I assume was to you. When I wished them a good morning, they broke apart very prettily, and I had to keep myself from laughing. Yet I believe that I must have a word with our sister. — EABD

Aside – Quite Interesting

From Georgiana Darcy to Fitzwilliam Darcy

Pemberley
Derbyshire
August 24

My Dearest Brother,

Greetings from Pemberley. I miss you terribly, and I know that dear Elizabeth is pining for you, though she presents a brave face to me and to Kitty. Even Kitty misses you, I believe, since her sister is less fun now that you are not here, and Kitty adores fun, as you know.

I shall not let Kitty know that you think her sister more beautiful than she, however, for no matter how well she might understand rationally that *of course* you should find your wife the most becoming of ladies, yet no young woman of my acquaintance likes to hear such things, even about her beloved sister. (You flatter me excessively concerning my own looks, accomplishments, and intelligence, and so my own pride feels no sting, I promise you.)

Yet even so, both Kitty and I find your doting upon Elizabeth and her doting upon you most sweet. She and I have talked (or, if I am being precise, *giggled*) about how like a pair of young lovers from one of our favourite books our brother and sister are.

As to those books — or rather, one book in particular, and the one that dear Elizabeth had overheard us reading — I have a confession to make to you, dear brother. It is M de Laclos's *Les Liaisons dangereuses,* which I believe our late cousin to have brought with him when he escaped Paris. I know that the book is, perhaps, a bit less *polite* than those you might prefer me to read. Kitty and I found the book in the library the very day of your departure, began to read it together as a way of practicing our French, and have been enjoying reading it together ever since. I hope you do not disapprove of the book or of our reading it. If you do, we shall of course cease at once.

As it happens, yesterday, Augustina and Tommy where here with a friend, Miss Godwin (who is indeed, as you say, *"quite interesting"*), and we began to read the book together — but Tommy complained that he could not follow the French, and asked us to read it in English, and so we were able to do just as you had suggested in your letter and include Elizabeth. She seemed to enjoy the book, but was taken with a terrible headache and retreated to her (or rather her and your) bedchamber.

Nonetheless, we have done our best to include my new sister in as many of our activities as we can, and while Kitty may indeed enjoy teasing Elizabeth at every opportunity — as she seems to tease everyone at all times — yet I believe that Kitty too is happy to have her sister join us. We went on quite an adventure into the woods the other day, and visited Mrs. Grouse there. It was a remarkable visit, and, as always with our old nurse, very educational.

By the way, I am quite touched that Kitty has taken to calling me *Gigi.* At first it was something of a shock, I will confess, since aside from Mrs. Grouse herself the only persons to have bestowed a pet name upon me were Mrs. Younge and that gentleman whose name we do not mention. And yet I have come to feel that it is a sign from her of friendship, and, more than that, of sisterhood. That I, who have been so blessed by a wonderful, caring brother, should now be further endowed with not one but two lovely new sisters by his marriage (three, if I include the lovely Mrs. Bingley) — I consider myself the luckiest of girls.

Then again, I have always considered myself so, having you for a brother and you and cousin Darcy (Cnl Fitzwilliam, I should say) as my guardians.

However, if you consider it improper or indecorous for me to allow the familiarity from Miss Bennet, I shall ask her to desist.

Likewise, if you think that I should encourage Master Giniver to cease his attentions toward Kitty, I shall ask Augustina to prevail upon him.

You know how I feel about Thomas, as we have discussed his past indiscretion with me. I have spoken with Augustina about it, and she assures me that her brother did not mean to frighten me so. Her belief is that their parents' opposite natures, combined with being the *young master* at Langley Park and with spending most of his youth at a school where no ladies were present, have led to him having no sense of proper behaviour with regard to members of the fairer sex. I must credit Augustina's opinion, for she knows him as well as anyone, and it fits all that I have observed about the future Lord Malkin. He clearly *likes us,* very much, and so feels moved to *kiss us* (as he attempted with me) or to *touch us*, as he has apparently done with some few of the servants, and yet few feel that they can rebuff his attentions as I did. Augustina argues that it is a strange kind of innocence in him, not malice. If this is indeed the case, it makes it easier for me to forgive, but no easier to trust him.

In any case, I believe that we need not worry that he will so leap over the bounds of polite behaviour as to compromise Kitty, not because he does not feel moved to do so (since he seems strongly drawn to her), but because she will not let him, and he seems to understand and respect her wishes. Perhaps he is growing more mature and less wild? We can hope so. I do not dislike Tommy, as I have said — but it is difficult not to distrust his actions (if not his intent).

Kitty treats him rather as I have seen Young Grouse treat puppies when he is training them for the hunt — sternly but lovingly. And Tommy seems to respond to the training with the same enthusiasm as the pups.

Even so, my new sister Elizabeth and I are both most careful not to leave them completely to their privacy, even as you suggested. Augustina too is very aware of her brother's propensity for misadventure, and does try to keep an eye out, but as you know she can be distracted by her enthusiasms.

She told us just yesterday of a most interesting discovery made recently by an Italian gentleman concerning the effect of *electricity* upon dead flesh. It was a fascinating conversation, even if it may have been less than precisely decorous. I do not think that aunt Catherine should have approved of the subject at all, thinking it *unladylike*, and I believe that it might have forced cousin Anne to take to her bed, as she so often seems compelled to do. Miss Godwin, Elizabeth, and I enjoyed it enormously, however.

As to the *attentions* of Lady Malkin, Kitty and I will do our best to keep the two Elizabeths from coming too directly in conflict. I do not know how much we can do, since Lady Malkin has seemed to show a great interest in your new bride. We have not seen the Countess for some days, so perhaps they shall come to their own *understanding?* Kitty and I shall do what we can, nonetheless.

As I said, I miss you terribly as well, dear brother — though not as terribly as Elizabeth does, I think.

The weather here has been glorious, after a few days of heavy rain. It is bright and sunny, but not too hot. I am sorry that London is so stifling at the moment. I hope that you are nonetheless enjoying the pleasures of the town?

We have discussed my own sense of unreadiness to *come out*. I believe that, after the passage of time since those terrible events of which we do not speak, and through the presence of your wife and of her sister (as well, of course, as the wonderful Mrs. Annesly, who writes to tell me that her sister-in-law is now happily delivered of a healthy boy, and who should return within a week or possibly two), that perhaps I may soon be ready to dare the Season. The thought still fills me with a kind of panic, but I believe that it is time for me to cease to behave as a young girl, as a *domina-in-potentia*, but to enter the world as a *young lady*. Augustina, who is nearly a year my junior, tells me that her parents may present her at court this winter, or perhaps next.

I know it is little time to launch me upon the seas of Society this year, yet perhaps we may plan for me to make my *début* at the same time as Miss Giniver?

The idea of doing so still fills me with cold terror, and yet I know it is what I must do, for you, for our family, and for myself.

That it is how I may find a *husband*, an eventuality for which I do not feel even vaguely ready — that possibility I cannot consider too deeply without it filling me with dread.

I know that I shall marry, and I look forward to the day. I am, as you know, as susceptible to tales of love and romance as any girl of my age.

Yet there is no man whom I have met who inspires in me the kind of fierce devotion that I see in you toward Elizabeth or in her toward you. And it is difficult for me, dear brother, to "*trust my own discernment*," as you suggest, when I was so nearly, so disastrously, and so easily led astray before.

I suppose that I dream that I may find a *friend*, who shall become a *husband*. I know that you and Elizabeth had some disagreements and troubles in your early friendship, yet I cannot imagine a better path to love and marriage. The idea of attempting to find such a *friend* among the metropolitan crowd at a string of balls and assemblies, exhibitions and performances — that I struggle to imagine. Yet I know that it is the most accepted way for a young woman of our station to find a husband, and so I shall attempt it.

As to my *friendship* with young John, or *Junkets*, as he insists we call him, he has been nothing but respect itself toward me, and I have done my best to maintain all the bounds of modesty and propriety in our interactions. We have been alone only once, and that was but for a moment when he delivered your letter to me, and aside from that he has only attended upon me when we are in company.

This evening, Kitty and I listened to him reading from Chapman's *Homer*, which you know is a favourite of mine. The book left him in such raptures that it was difficult not to be swept along with him. When Elizabeth joined us, she too found his passion for the translation moving, and so gifted the volume to him, which seemed to delight him even more than it delighted me. Dear brother, if you have the opportunity, would you mind buying a new copy of this wonderful translation while you are in town? I should greatly appreciate it, and I believe that your wife would as well.

In any case, I shall do as you ask, as always. I, like you, enjoy Junkets's company — he shared some lovely poems that he has written with me and with Kitty — but I shall, as always, keep our exchanges within all of the bounds of propriety. I do not believe that he will do otherwise.

I look forward to hearing from you again, but even more to seeing you.

Your loving sister,

Georgiana Darcy

12 – A Midsummer Fancy

From Fitzwilliam Darcy to Elizabeth Darcy

Nr 12, Berkeley Sqr
London
August 26

My Dearest Mrs. Darcy Mother Goose, ~~and~~ Lady Swan,

I see.

I am indeed no gander but a goose, though yet no father, as you have shown me. I have never been so happy to show myself a fool.

I might blame my folly upon Lady Malkin's hints concerning Augustina's paternity, yet in truth the mistake is mine alone, and was already established before she began to play upon my fears. The timing of her pregnancy with Augustina came so hard on the period of our own liaisons that I can say that my mistake was natural, and does make me wonder whether she might have deliberately resumed her intimacies with her husband so as to make me mistake so — or perhaps to cover her own putative shame, should she find herself unexpectedly with child by me, by George Wickham, or by some other fellow concupiscent.

Her purpose in telling you a tale of her own childhood lifted from a somewhat notorious (though *quite interesting*) French novel — that I cannot tell. It is as likely that she was simply enjoying a joke at your expense as that she was actively attempting to gain your sympathy. It may, I suppose, have been an attempt to achieve both objectives at once. Or it may have been for some other reason altogether, some reason clear only to her.

If Grouse does not shoot the lady when next she enters our grounds, I promise you, I shall do it myself.

In any case, thank you, *ladodi, mon amour, agapimeni mou, meine liebeling, amata mei,* for removing the blinkers from my eyes and leading me out of the waste land of my folly. Indeed, I needed only to consider the portraits at Pemberley and those at Langley (not to mention those at my uncle's Annesly Hall) to see what you meant. What kind of husband-man am I indeed, not to have seen what should have been so clear? When we speak with the farmers who manage and breed our cattle, I shall leave the business to you, my country wife, since I am clearly incompetent in such matters.

I am blessed with a wife of unparalleled beauty — but also of unparalleled perspicacity, unparalleled compassion, and unparalleled passion too, as I am fortunate enough to know well. I now see, in addition, that you are truly *sans pareil* with regards to your forgiveness, your cleverness, and also your unrelenting good humor. You are a treasure, Elizabeth Darcy, and the treasure's guardian as well, and Pemberley is scarcely grand enough a setting for such a jewel.

I am very aware that Mrs. Grouse is an excellent healer, not only of women's complaints, but of all the neighborhood's.

I am aware too that women who do not wish themselves to be with child might seek means of *taking care of the trouble.* That Mrs. Grouse might provide such means I did not know, but I suppose I am not surprised.

I do not know how I feel, morally and ethically, about such questions. Even so, since the near tragedy at Ramsgate and last summer's tragedy averted at Brighton, I have become very conscious of the unequal weight of consequence that *carnal embrace, &c.* lays upon women as opposed to men.

Yet the idea of taking such actions does leave me ill at ease.

I suppose it is a good thing, then, that we have all our lives ahead of us, since there is much of import for us to discuss and debate. I look forward to it immensely.

Of your maid, I shall say nothing, except to grant that I am disappointed — as you say, Miss Gwynn has always seemed a very sensible girl. You seem to have handled her situation with your usual grace and care.

Concerning Master Giniver, I share your disquiet. Georgiana has written me that his actions are less the result of vice than of inexperience. She tells me too that your sister has him well in hand — that she is training him, to use Georgiana's image, as our gamekeeper trains his pups. If it be so, then perhaps all shall end well, yet.

Like you, however, I am most uncertain that his parents would approve of such a match. Lady Malkin may be the daughter herself of a merchant (though of an Austrian *Gräfin* as well, as she told you), yet she has always seemed to set great store by station. That would seem to be her only point of commonality with Lady Catherine, my aunt. Lord Malkin, on the other hand, has never seemed to hold distinction of rank at a particularly high rate. I do not know what he would think of his son courting Kitty.

As you say, it may yet prove a midsummer fancy, as brief and insubstantial as a dream. Let us remain wary then, but not yet interfere.

When I first met your sister Catherine, I will admit that I did not think her given to much substance. I now see that, while she is merry to a fault (though I will not dismiss her as your father does as *utterly silly*), she does seem to have her own hidden strengths — a generosity of spirit and well-concealed sense of cleverness among them. Perhaps she and Thomas shall bring out the best in each other?

Or perhaps we may thank my sister *Gigi* for encouraging your sister Kitty's good sense, even as Kitty encourages in Georgiana a more merry sensibility.

Georgiana assures me, by the way, that she and Junkets are staying most strictly within the bounds of propriety.

She tells me too (as you had already done) of how you gave our Cupid the first folio copy of the Chapman translation of *The Odysseys of Homer* — a volume that had enriched the shelves of the Pemberley library since the house's earlier, Tudor incarnation, very nearly two hundred years ago. Well, my beloved, I see that in addition to your famous beauty, modesty, and intelligence, that you shall be famous in your magnanimity as well.

What a princely gift!

(It seems I do not have your capacity to tease, or, at least, that I do not take the pleasure in holding up the jest that your father's daughters all seem to do. The book is but a book. That you gave it to one who clearly can love and appreciate it — and to one who has, as you say, done us great service — seems just and proper. He showed me the book himself, and seemed quite overwhelmed by your generosity in giving it to him.)

I too am sad that your *monthly visitor* came and gave the truth to Mrs. Grouse's prognosis. Yet this gives us the opportunity to essay again, my love, and I am more impatient to make the attempt than I believe I can express.

[Discolouration]

Here is yet more fresh evidence of my desire for you. I know that your thoughts are not now as given to fleshly pleasures as at another time of the month, yet I could not withhold sharing it with you.

It was inspired by the daydream that you described, two letters ago, of you, doffing your chemise, and approaching me, waiting, on the bed. When next you do that in person, I hope that I shall last longer than I have just now, and if I do not, I hope that you will forgive me.

We *have* taken possession of the *mansion of our love* — though as you say, we yet have many rooms, out-buildings, fields, and woods to fully occupy. I look forward to occupying each and every one with you.

I am now imagining your gracious form rising like Venus from the lake below the house. Do you like to swim, Mrs. Darcy?

I am happy to have you shoulder any burden that I carry, save the light one of caring for you. My business here is almost concluded, and I look forward to leaving the city no later than the week-end. I shall see you before the calendar turns, if the gods (and the roads) be willing.

In any case, my love, you are no goose, but a swan.

Faithfully, foolishly, and ferociously,
Yours,

Father Goose

PS We must play Tom o' Straw in the eastern fields below the lake when

I return. We should wait until the grain is harvested, however, since, as you say, the farmers' wrath at trampled wheat should be terrible indeed, and I should not wish to incur it, even for so pleasant a game. (I believe that the farmer of those fields where Miss Gwynn and Master Giniver *disported* themselves is in fact Miss Gwynn's father.) — FG

PPS I shall go anywhere you wish, in Lancashire or London. Indeed, I shall promise to go to a ball with you, and though I do not love to dance, I should love to dance *with you*. Indeed, we may have an opportunity to do so soon, since, in her letter to me, Georgiana told me that she might be willing to *dare the Season*. This rather astonished me, since she has until now been vehement in her refusal so to expose herself to Society. Please, if you might let my sister know that I have begun to answer some of her thoughts, and shall send a response when next Junkets rides north. I would not delay his rounds just now, however. — FG

PPPS Also, please let Georgiana know that, while I do find the book that she, Catherine, and Augustina have been reading to be rather less than *proper* for a group of cultured young ladies, I do not object to their continuing to read from it — but only if you are present and they continue to translate. In such manner, they may continue their practice of the French language, and, should there be any passages that cause them inordinate *distress*, you will be able to answer any questions and clarify any obscure points.

PPPPS I cannot now read this aloud to you, and yet I cannot wait to share it, since it expresses my desires better than I could myself:

> *Come, Madam, come, all rest my powers defy,*
> *Until I labour, I in labour lie.*
> *The foe oft-times having the foe in sight,*
> *Is tir'd with standing though he never fight.*
> *Off with that girdle, like heaven's Zone glistering,*
> *But a far fairer world encompassing.*
> *Unpin that spangled breastplate which you wear,*
> *That th'eyes of busy fools may be stopped there.*
> *Unlace yourself, for that harmonious chime,*

Tells me from you, that now it is bed time.
Off with that happy busk, which I envy,
That still can be, and still can stand so nigh.
Your gown going off, such beauteous state reveals,
As when from flowery meads th'hill's shadow steals.
Off with that wiry Coronet and shew
The hairy Diadem which on you doth grow:
Now off with those shoes, and then safely tread
In this love's hallow'd temple, this soft bed.
In such white robes, heaven's Angels used to be
Received by men; Thou Angel bringst with thee
A heaven like Mahomet's Paradise; and though
Ill spirits walk in white, we easily know,
By this these Angels from an evil sprite,
Those set our hairs, but these our flesh upright.
Licence my roving hands, and let them go,
Before, behind, between, above, below.
O my America! my new-found-land,
My kingdom, safeliest when with one man mann'd,
My Mine of precious stones, My Empirie,
How blest am I in this discovering thee!
To enter in these bonds, is to be free;
Then where my hand is set, my seal shall be.
Full nakedness! All joys are due to thee,
As souls unbodied, bodies uncloth'd must be,
To taste whole joys. Gems which you women use
Are like Atlanta's balls, cast in men's views,
That when a fool's eye lighteth on a Gem,
His earthly soul may covet theirs, not them.
Like pictures, or like books' gay coverings made
For lay-men, are all women thus array'd;
Themselves are mystic books, which only we
(Whom their imputed grace will dignify)
Must see reveal'd. Then since that I may know;
As liberally, as to a Midwife, shew
Thy self: cast all, yea, this white linen hence,
There is no penance due to innocence.
To teach thee, I am naked first; why then
What needst thou have more covering than a man.

Aside – The Canker Gnawing

From Margaret Gardiner to Elizabeth Darcy

Gracechurch Street, *Aug. 26*

My dear Niece,

I am delighted to hear from you, dear Lizzy. Yes, you do seem to have been rather distracted of late, and I simply cannot think of a reason why, myself.

In truth, I should not have anticipated a letter from you until the snows fall there in green Derbyshire. I expected you to be utterly lost in daily (and hourly) *experimentation* with your beautiful, attentive husband.

Were he not here in London, I should have cause to worry indeed that you have answered my letter so soon!

I shall not make this letter long, since I know that you had much rather be pining for the husband that our City has stolen from you.

I am glad too that you found some of my suggestions *helpful*. I know that (as much as it embarrassed me) the wisdom that my mother and my sister Susan (may they rest in peace) shared with me before my wedding to your wonderful uncle Edward did much to calm me — and to enrich our early experiences of one another. And since I feared you could scarcely count on your mother for such assistance nor your sister Lydia (who may have been the first married, but yet is the least mature of my nieces), I chose to share my store of wifely knowledge with you.

The particular suggestion that you mentioned has been a special favourite of Edward's — and of mine too, especially during my courses. And when we were first married, I had even less to press together there than you do, my dear, I assure you.

The suggestion that I believe I put last in the letter — of pleasing one another simultaneously with tongue and lip, like a pair of hoop snakes attempting to devour one another — I highly encourage you to try, if your husband is willing. It is perhaps more acrobatic than many of the other forms of embrace that I mentioned, yet Edward and I have always found it to be among the most mutually pleasurable — especially when we are *not* trying to produce more children at the moment, as you may some day come to wish.

As I write that, I am sure that you are squirming uncomfortably, attempting not to think of me and of your uncle in such an embrace. If so, I apologise; it will be many years before I can share this store of knowledge with sweet Joan, and by that point I hope that she will have a far more accomplished (and welcome) tutor in her cousin Elizabeth. Therefor I shall disregard any scruples you might be having in order to spare my own and my daughter's discomfort once our eldest is of an age to require these lessons.

Mr. Darcy was kind enough to join us in Cheapside once again this evening for supper. Oh, Lizzy, he truly is a most gracious and handsome man. And I see that I was correct: he wanted nothing to make him quite perfect but a prudent marriage and the love of a *lively* wife, both of which seem to have settled upon him most happily. Know that he is as anxious to return to you as you are anxious for him to do so. I am certain that he has told you this himself, but perhaps it bears repeating.

As to the *canker gnawing at your bud*, of course I did not mind that you unburdened your worries to me — I hope that you will always feel that you may do so.

I do understand your discomfort. It is hard to think of one's husband with another, I know. Though your uncle had not been intimate with other women before our marriage — at least, not in the carnal sense — yet there was a young lady named Harriet in Meryton with whom he had shared some affection before leaving to make his fortune in the City. He told me about her very early on, all full of guilt, and I absolved him utterly.

Yet she was a friend of your aunt Phillips, and so on the occasion when I first visited Hertfordshire with my new husband, this Harriet was introduced to me. And while I could accept his having known girls before he knew me (as he accepted my having known some Lambton boys), meeting the woman — also happily married and with two children at the time — filled me with unreasoning spasms of jealousy.

I wish that I could say that there were any magical method for dispelling *the green-eyed monster,* but I am afraid that the only way for me to get past the spasm was to love and trust my husband, and to allow him to love and trust me. I have been shaken with such spasms from time to time since. After Alfreda's birth, I had as you may remember a particularly difficult and lengthy lying-in, yet your uncle was required to leave on business, just as your husband has done. I was certain that I was ugly and worn, no longer attractive to him or to anyone, and that he was seeking other, livelier company out in the country. Now, he had shown, as always, his continued devotion in many, many ways, and yet I could not rid myself of the doubt. When he returned, I was sure that I should find letters or tokens of his loves (for I was sure that there were many) in his bags — yet I found not a thing.

I then had to make a decision: either to trust the man I love, or to distrust him. I chose to trust him, since he had never given me any sign of unfaithfulness, nor has he in the years since. For to distrust him would have been to throw away all that we had built together.

Choose, Lizzy: do you wish to trust your husband? If you do, *tell him of your feelings.* He will think no less of you for them, unless I miss my mark.

You have a wonderful husband, my dear, and he has a wonderful wife. The more you show each other, not only love and passion and all of the positive things that you share, but also anger and frustration and, yes, even jealousy, the stronger your marriage shall be. You did promise, did you not, to be together *for better and for worse, in richer and in poorer, in sickness and in health, so long as ye both shall live?*

A good marriage is begun by enjoying the *better,* but is strengthened by overcoming the *worse.* All marriages have their difficulties, and when the team *pulls in tandem,* even over rough road, then the marriage can survive all hazards and flourish.

As has mine to your uncle, and as I know that yours will to Mr. Darcy.

I shared your greeting with the children just now, and they all asked to be remembered to you, and to ask when they could visit and ride the pony. (Edward tells me his pony riding days are behind him, alas.) Freddie in particular asks whether she can take home the rabbit that she found in the Pemberley Woods; I told her that she would make the poor bun's family very sad to take it away so, but she informed me that *her cousin* was the Mistress of Pemberley and she would order Mr. Bunny to go with her. I believe she thinks you to be the Queen of Derbyshire, and perhaps she is right.

M. Gardiner

13 – Come Home, Darcy

From Elizabeth Darcy to Fitzwilliam Darcy

Pemberley, Derbyshire, *August 26/27*

PLEASE, DARCY, READ THE LAST PART
OF THIS LETTER FIRST, FOR IT IS URGENT

My dearest Darcy,

Once Junkets rode off yesterday morning with two letters and a book of Homer in the lockbox in his horse's saddlebags, I wandered the halls of Pemberley, at a strange loose end. There were no Ginivers, no odd Mary, no invitation to Langley Park (thankfully), and Kitty and Georgiana went to walk about the lake. (They promised me that they would not leave the estate, and if they met up with any visitors they would bring them straight back to the house. My sister I might not trust to follow such an injunction to the letter, but Georgiana I would trust to obey implicitly.)

Jane and Charles are in Hertfordshire — or perhaps our mother has already driven them to London. The servants were all very busy with the work of keeping our beautiful house beautiful (among other things — but more on that later). No one had any need of me.

And so I went to continue to introduce myself to the family portraits, having used them without their permission in my last letter to you.

Today, I spoke with Lady Anne, your mother. May I say that I have never seen anyone (aside possibly from Georgiana) who so manages to typify my ideas both of *dark* and of *fair?*

She was even more gracious than your father in forgiving me all of my multifold, manifold shortcomings. She told me that you had been a most delightful baby, which I can believe. She told me that while she regretted not having been able to watch you and Georgiana grow to adulthood, yet she would not trade having given birth to you both for all the world. That she was proud of whom you had both become.

She *was* somewhat scandalised when I told her that I wished to feed our children at my own breast, rather than at a local woman's — even so remarkable a woman as Mrs. Grouse (who seems almost certainly past being able to nurse, in any case).

However surprised she may have been, your mother informed me that she understood my desire, and should happily accept it — were you of like mind.

How can such a lady as your mother have been sister to such a lady as your aunt? Perhaps I am giving to much credit to a portrait, yet the woman I beheld in that lovely painting seemed as gracious and warm as her sister has always struck me as cutting and cold.

And perhaps, too, I am giving too much credence to blood, for do I not have both Mary and Lydia as my own sisters?

In the afternoon, I retired to the library, where I found Mr. Chapman's *Iliad*. I do not enjoy the book anywhere nearly as much as *The Odyssey*, yet the translation remains lucid and lovely, and so I am enjoying the language, even if all of the characters seem like a group of petulant boys, playing at a game far less entertaining than Tom-o'-Straw. Achilles, in particular, seems like the kind of loutish bully who always spoiled everyone's fun when he did not win.

Perhaps if they all listened to the women, they would be less ridiculous.

Mrs. Reynolds came and informed me that the malt was ready, and would be delivered to The Spotted Lamb on the day of the wedding (which is this Saturday) and that I could present the gift to Miss Lewis whenever I should like — though it would be best if it were done in the next day or two, since Miss Lewis is naturally leaving our employ on Friday. I suggested that it should be handled immediately, which the housekeeper felt was an excellent choice (and clearly the one that she had intended I should make — I wonder, sometimes, at how much our servants *manage* us). I then asked her to send Miss Lewis up to me, and also to tell me where I might lay hands on the famous gold sovereign, since I realised that I have not had to carry any money this past month.

She gave me the coin (which I am sure that she had secreted in one of the many pockets of her apron for just this purpose) and went to call the kitchen maid to the library.

As she left me, I realised with a start that yesterday we had been married a month — and were not together to mark the occasion. The thought filled me with a surplus of sorrow — sorrow at your being gone, sorrow at our losing these precious days. It is silly, I will grant (I am once again Mother Goose), yet all I could think of as I sat there, the volume of violent ends and unexpected partings lying in my lap, was that we have a numbered limit to our days together, and though we cannot know how large that number may be (and I dearly hope that it shall be very, very large), that I cannot help but mourn the loss of each not spent together.

It was as I was wallowing in these rather maudlin thoughts that Miss Lewis came in to speak with me. I did my best to smile, which was not too hard to do, since I am happy for our kitchen maid, handed her the gold coin with our congratulations, and informed her of the bushels of malted barley that would be delivered to the inn in time for her wedding.

She thanked me, and began to weep, saying we were too kind, that the Darcys' generosity was already well-known, but that I was clearly cut from the same cloth. That as much as she was looking forward to her wedding, the thought of the life after was filling her with uncertainty, and our gift reminded her that all would be well.

And so, of course, *I* began to weep, and we stood there, both of us crying, two young women overwhelmed by feelings quite beyond the actual conversation.

Once we had both managed to calm ourselves somewhat, we talked for a while. She thanked me for my little improvised paean in the kitchens to the joys of married life, and said that it had helped her much over the past week as her own wedding approached and her nerves began to get the better of her.

I told her that I was very glad — that everyone I knew that had got married felt just such a crisis of nerve on approaching so momentous a change of life (excepting Lydia, of course, who seems to have approached it, like everything, as a child's game). And for some reason I began to cry again.

Fanny Lewis looked at me, her broad, raw face uncomfortably knowing, and said, "Aye, th'art missing t'Master, isn't'ee?"

When I granted that yes, I was missing you rather terribly, she nodded and said, "I canno' blame'ee. He's a good'un, Master Darcy. I's been in the kitchens here since I's a girl, and I's ne'er heard a course word said again'im. And he is handsome and all."

I granted that this, too, was very true.

"And I'm sure he's good t'thee… in private and all." And then she began to blush and apologise for having presumed, but I actually found myself laughing, and saying that yes, indeed, you were *very* good to me in private, as I hoped her husband would be to her.

She thanked me again, and said, "Mistress Darcy, when'ee first came t'house, many of us feared'ee couldn't be worthy o't'Master, for many o'us were sure none could be. But thee's been a good mistress, and good t'Master Darcy. Us's all very glad thee's become Mistress o' Pemberley."

And that, of course, set us both weeping again.

When we had calmed ourselves and each other once again, Miss Lewis told me that she needed to return to the kitchens — that there were fish to scale and gut and bacon to slice — and that there would be a small banquet in her honour in the servants' hall that night to mark her departure. I asked if I might intrude, and she said that, while she wouldn't wish to presume upon my time, that I should of course be welcome — as I would always be welcome at the inn when she was mistress there.

I had just returned to reading about Agamemnon and Achilles arguing over who *owns* the maid Briseis, like a pair of boys fighting over a prized conker, when our sisters entered with guests. I was surprised to see not the ever-so-redheaded Giniver siblings, but Mr. Shelley and Miss Godwin. Mr. Shelley informed me that they were on their way to catch a coach to London, to see Miss Godwin's father, to inform Mr. Godwin of Mr. Shelley's intent to leave his wife and marry Mary.

This was the first that I had heard of Mr. Shelley being married. As he spoke very excitedly with Kitty and Georgiana (who both seemed reasonably non-plussed by the revelation, but managed to listen politely to the poet), I asked Mary, whom I have come to like, for all that she is decidedly odd, whether she was sure of this course of action. She answered that, as she had told me, she had always meant to marry Percy, and repeated her intention to bear his children and love him beyond the bounds of death itself.

She then thanked me for my hospitality, and said that, when she wrote her first novel, the heroine would be a radiant beauty with exquisite eyes named Elizabeth.

I was, as I'm sure you can imagine, rather astonished by this, and said that, when she wrote it, I should love to read it, whatever the heroine's name.

It is a strange thing: Mr. Shelley is a noted and published poet, while his intended (second) bride is scarcely more than a girl, yet I believe that she will indeed write something, and that it shall be remarkable. And whether or not the heroine should bear my name (which is, now that I think on it, also the name of Mary's hostess at Langley Park), I shall look forward to reading it.

They then took their leave, returning to the Malkin phaeton that was waiting to whisk them away to Lambton and the London Post Coach.

I thanked our sisters for doing as they had promised and bringing the visitors to me immediately. (I did not point out that, if it had been Tommy and Augustina, I was sure that the trip from the lake to the house might have been less direct and of longer duration.)

We all then took a walk, not toward the lake, where Kitty and Georgiana had spent the day, but into the beautiful woods, toward the lookout where we might watch the sunset over the whole of the valley.

We saw no one — not even my ghostly servant — though someone (I am assuming Young Grouse) seemed to have been digging at the bases of many of the trees. We watched the setting of the sun with pleasure, and then returned to Pemberley just in time for our own supper. I informed the girls of Miss Lewis's invitation to the banquet below stairs, and so as soon as we had eaten the meal that Mrs. Patchett, Miss Lewis, & Co had prepared for us, we three trooped down to the servants' hall, where the staff's own supper was merrily underway. As we entered, the room quietened, but Miss Lewis (soon to be Mrs. Lennon) stood, red-cheeked, and welcomed us to the party. She then proposed a toast to the Darcys — including their newest members. There was much banging of cutlery upon the tables and cries of "Hear, hear!" Mugs of ale were placed in our hands, and the whole assembly — myself and our sisters included — drank deeply to the health and prosperity of the Darcy house. (The beer was very bitter, but refreshing, and in the warm room was quite delightful. Hill brewed ale at Longbourn — mostly for the servants — and would occasionally sneak us a sip. Her ale was sweeter and *darker* than this, and I believe somewhat less potent, as you will see.)

The senior staff — Mr. and Mrs. Reynolds, Mrs. Patchett, and Mr. Norton the steward — all went about and refilled everyone's ale from huge jugs. I found myself thinking that I should help them, but when I went to do so, I was told in no uncertain terms that our sisters and I were guests in the hall (for all that we owned it), and should enjoy ourselves.

Inspired (possibly by the ale) I then proposed a toast to Miss Lewis, to her imminent marriage, and to the enduring joys of matrimony. This evoked another loud cheer from the hall, and another deep toast was quaffed off.

Kitty, Georgiana and I found ourselves sitting with Florry and a pair of housemaids, to whom Georgiana introduced us — I believe their names were Ursula (she seems to be Florry's sister) and Margaret, if you can credit that. We discussed the coming wedding, but I will have to be honest with you: their Derbyshire accents were so marked that Kitty and I could understand at best one word in three — even Florry's. This amused them terribly. At one point, I believe Georgiana (who could understand them better) was talking with them about Augustina's *galvanic post*. At least, I believe that's what they were discussing. In any case, it caused much mirth.

We stayed but a little while more — I did not wish to dampen the staff's merriment — and returned upstairs. Kitty and Georgiana were more than a bit red-cheeked, as, I am sure, I was myself. We bid each other good night, and I retired to our chamber. I had intended to write to you, but apparently fell asleep still in my gown. I woke to find Florry

— rather loudly and unsteadily — entering our chamber, and then attempting to get me undressed and into bed.

I will admit that I have rarely actually felt the need for assistance in that regard more than I did last night. Unfortunately, Florry was herself less than usually effective in her aid.

I have some memory of asking about her sister and Margaret — and then asking where Hero and Beatrice had got to, which confused poor Florry completely. What happened after that I am uncertain. And so I woke this morning to find myself completely unclothed, with the linen shift in which I have usually slept bunched under my head as a pillow. Also, Florry was snoring on the floor.

Once I had woken Florry, bathed, and dressed, I stumbled down to breakfast.

Though it was past eight o'clock, the staff were only just beginning to stir. They were all well-scrubbed and the food as excellent as ever, but it was not difficult to see that all were slower than is their wont. I did not begrudge them in the slightest, since I was happy that they should have properly celebrated Miss Lewis's upcoming nuptials.

Mrs. Reynolds did not make her usual appearance at the breakfast table. Mr. Reynolds, the butler, instead presided. I asked him how late the carousing lasted into the night and he informed me that it was moderately late, but that he had assured the staff that we above stairs would not mind if the morning should start a touch later than usual, since we were there — for at least a part of the festivities.

Georgiana came in, looking her usual, polished self. I asked if she had seen Kitty, and she informed me that Kitty was feeling a bit *tired*, and would be down later, which I am afraid caused me to laugh. It was not terribly generous of me, I know.

As we ate, Georgiana shared your letter to her, and told me of her letter to you.

I think that you were *very sweet* to ask that she and Kitty take care of me — and also *very sly* to ask that they include me in their reading of naughty novels. I see my forthright, upstanding husband has a somewhat duplicitous side; I shall watch you all the more carefully, my dear husband.

And because I know you this well, at least, I know that you shall now assure me that you were *not* duplicitous; that your request was honestly meant, even if it did also serve our purposes. My love, I know you to be honest to an absolute fault. I am teasing you. However, I am impressed that you managed to pull off such a stratagem without in any way stooping to dishonesty. You might have made a wonderful woman, husband, though I am very glad that you are as you are. I should miss your cock (*battering ram, upstanding member,* et cetaera,) most terribly.

In any case, thanks to Miss Godwin (or Mrs. Shelley, as she hopes soon to be), I was included in the reading without your scheme, though thanks to it I feel sure that they will continue to allow me to listen.

I find myself wondering whether Mr. Godwin will extend his philosophy of free-love to his daughter? How shall he feel about her marrying a man who is leaving his previous wife? And how should the young lady's late mother feel on the subject? I am uncertain whether I wish the peculiar couple well or not, for all that I do rather like odd Mary. Mr. Shelley is, I am afraid, a bit of a cad, and that is quite beside the fact that I am not terribly fond of his poetry.

Georgiana told me, too, of her asking about going to London for the Season this winter or next. She wondered what I might think of this.

It was at this point that Kitty stumbled in looking rather like a bear stuffed into a muslin morning gown. Opening just one eye as she collapsed into the chair, she asked, "Are we going to London?"

Knowing that our father has no intention of setting my sister adrift in *those* treacherous waters, and guessing from her tentative approach to the subject that Georgiana had at best mixed feelings on the subject, I assured her that at the moment *we* were going nowhere, that our sister-in-law was merely considering when and how best to come out, and that from what you had written to your sister, now was *not* a time to be in London, in any case.

Though, as you know, I should follow you there in an instant, if I could but travel on Signor Galvani's *electrical ether.*

But I am a good and dutiful wife (or at least, I am attempting to be so), and so here among the Arcadian glories of Pemberley I shall stay. Oh, woe is me!

I attempted to draw out Georgiana on the subject of her *coming out,* but Kitty's presence seemed to have left your sister less willing to open up, and my sister, as she will do, began to fill the silence with prattle

— about the feast in the servants' hall last night and the taste of the ale, about how the maid assigned to her had abandoned her this morning.

When I asked her whether the drapes to her bed and windows had been drawn when she woke, and whether her chamber pot had been full, Kitty frowned and said that the maid must have forgot to close them last night.

Georgiana very diplomatically suggested that she herself had slept more than usually soundly after the previous evening's merriment, and that perhaps Kitty had slept through the maid's arrival.

I laughed (again, not terribly kind of me), and agreed that this may very well have been the case, while Kitty scowled, bear-like once more, and ate her muffin and apricot jam and sipped at her much-sweetened tea in relative silence.

Once we had eaten and our moods were somewhat settled, Kitty suggested an outing to Langley Park. I was trying to think how to demur when Georgiana said that she had promised a letter to Mrs. Annesly, and could we perhaps go visit the Ginivers tomorrow?

Kitty granted that she too had several letters to write — to Mama, to Lydia, and to Maria Lucas (Charlotte's sister, whom you remember from our visit to Rosings). And so she granted that perhaps we could postpone a trip to Langley Park to the afternoon.

And so I have been writing this letter to you (and also one to my parents, whom I have not written in over a week). As I write, I have been trying to think how to avoid having to visit Lady Malkin's lair. Perhaps I can ask Mr. Reynolds to have all of the horses brought to the farrier? I am sure that they could stand to be reshod. And I can suggest to Mrs. Reynolds that all of *our* shoes need to be seen to as well.

You see, my dearest Darcy, though I may be forthright (since infancy, as my father apparently told you) and strive to be honest, I *am* capable of being somewhat duplicitous. I am not proud that this is so, yet so it is.

As it happens, however, my stratagems were unnecessary, for today at least. As I was finishing those last paragraphs, Florry entered to inform me that Master Tommy and Miss Augustina had arrived, that the whole of the company was reconvening in the library, and that my presence was requested.

As she came downstairs with me, I asked Florry whether she had fully recovered from her night on the floor. She rolled her eyes and informed me that she's slept on less comfortable beds than our rug, to which I replied that she was always welcome to sleep there — providing my husband was not present. She pertly noted that that would only allow her a few more days, and I realised that it was indeed August 26 — that the end of the month and your promised return were indeed almost nigh! I may yet survive this long separation of two weeks. How the wives of sea captains can stand it I cannot begin to think.

When I reached the library, Thomas was entreating our sisters to start at the beginning of *Perilous Meetings*, since he wished to understand all that was happening. His sister agreed, since she had not read the book for some time, and also would appreciate a fresh start. The vote being evenly split, the assembly turned to me. I said that I, like Tommy, would enjoy hearing the story from the beginning, and since the exercise was (at least in part) to practice their French, our sisters could profit from the repetition.

And so, somewhat shyly, they began at the beginning.

I see that I was right — it is a very interesting book, if as I said somewhat vulgar. The author makes wonderful use of the epistolary form to create the different characters. The Viscount is prideful, somewhat arrogant, but also charming. He reminds me of someone, but I cannot think who.

I should love to discuss it with you when you return.

The Ginivers left, having exacted a promise that we visit them tomorrow — a promise from which all of my stratagems and ploys cannot seem to release me.

I shall take up this letter when we return — *if* we return, and Lady Malkin and I have not fought a duel to the death with goose quills and spindles.

Indeed, I have returned, and to find the wonderful Junkets waiting for us!

The day at Langley Park was pleasant. Lady Malkin was not present, and so no debt of honour needed to be paid. We walked about the park with Tommy and Augustina, and enjoyed the beautiful new grounds — Augustina told us that Lord Malkin had the park completely replanted for Lady Malkin's delight. I found that lovely, but it struck me as odd that so urbane a person as Elizabeth Giniver should be pleased by such bucolic surroundings. It seems rather as if she has been *penned* there, and that made me *almost* feel for the lady.

We read some more of *Perilous Meetings*. I begin to see that the story is framed as a series of seductions, but also of romantic triangles, each of which calls into question the intentions of the various participants. I should love to find a copy in English to reread at my leisure, for the story is more intriguing than I think I could tell, starting from the middle.

Your letter made me smile, my love! I am sorry for ever making so wise and serious man feel foolish, since you are neither gander nor goose. Yet I am glad that you have so quickly seen why I could not take your fears seriously.

Yet I hope that we can make you a father, and soon indeed. I think you shall be an *excellent* father, not only since you are so clearly a good man and a good husband, but since I see the care which you have already shown your sister, and can see how well she has been raised.

As to my taking over discussions of husbandry with the farmers who manage the breeding of our cattle — well, my lord and husband, I should be only so happy to take such a burden from your shoulders, but you must train me further in the matter of *breeding*. I fear I am still to green in the practice of the act, though I may understand the theory. Will you undertake to complete my education?

And yes, husband, I do like to swim, though it goes without saying that I have not swum in the presence of *boys* since I was quite young. If you promise to dance with me, I shall promise to swim with you — and I believe that in this bargain, neither of us shall come out the loser.

I am now thinking of *you* rising, nude, from the lake — the water glistening as it streams from your skin, your eyes dark, liquid fire, promising to *burn* me with pleasure. The whole of you, like some perfect piece of Italian sculpture. Oh, Darcy, would you take me there, by the lakeside, with all the heavens as our witness?

[Discolouration]

There, my lord, is proof of how your mere imagined presence affects me. Even now, with my courses only just passed, you fill me with such longing that I fear I cannot stand to wait until the month's end and shall jump on Junkets's charger and ride post-haste to London, so that I may *ride you*.

Come home, Darcy, and *fuck me*, even as Dean Donne promised to do to his *mistress*, who is *safliest, when with one man manned.*

Before I combust completely, I shall take my evening stroll out to watch the sunset from the edge of the woods. I have no doubt that I shall have more unspent passion to share with you.

I must finish quickly and get this letter to Junkets immediately. *Something terrible has happened.*

I met Lady M in the woods as I walked. She was dressed in poor imitation of a servant — I have just realised that *hers* must be the spectral figure that I have spied in the woods these past days.

She was got up as noblewoman's idea of a maid — loose clothes in drab colours, yet of course well cut and of fine fabric. She carried a shovel and a bag and was digging at the base of a tree, some distance from the place where she and I had encountered Mrs. Grouse.

When I called out to her, she turned and made to flee — to hide, as she must have done on the previous occasions when I saw her — but I ran after her, and stopped her by grabbing the shovel.

I did not know what she intended, yet her actions were so ferocious and unexpected, and, if I am honest, I so distrusted the lady that I could not let her go without some explanation.

I asked her what she was digging for in our woods. She merely snarled at me like a cornered bitch and attempted to free the shovel from my grip.

While Lady Malkin may be my senior and my better, yet she is slight and city-bred. I tore the shovel from her.

Furious, she reached into her bag and withdrew what I saw was a birding pistol. Fearing she meant to shoot me (even as I had jokingly said in our letters that I meant to shoot her), I swung the newly liberated shovel and knocked the gun from her hand, causing it to discharge against the ground (very fortunately — I know that birdshot was unlikely to have killed her or me, yet it might have done terrible damage, and I should prefer not to be shot, thank you very much).

As Lady Malkin cradled her hand to her chest and looked about for some avenue of escape, I raised the shovel and demanded once more what she was doing on our property.

She laughed, and I must tell you, her laughter was more frightening than the earlier animal snarls had been. Her grey silk cap fallen to the ground, her hair and eyes were quite wild, and though she looked furious, her skin was as pale as a corpse's. "What do you *think* I am doing here, you stupid *cow!*"

"I think, *Elizabeth*," I said, as calmly as I could, "that you are looking for the death caps that Mrs. Grouse warned us of the other day."

Again, she laughed, and again it was a sound to make the hair on my arms stand on end.

"I can think of no good reason for you to do so," I continued, keeping the blade of the shovel raised so that she could neither attack nor flee. "I *fear* that you can only mean to kill someone, and I will not let you do it."

"*MY HUSBAND,*" she screamed, "*MY HUSBAND THE FUCKING LORD MALKIN KEEPS ME CAGED LIKE AN ANIMAL!*"

I gasped, realizing that I had jokingly made just such an observation in this very letter.

Her eyes narrowed. "Yes, yes, *Elizabeth,* he is so *kind* and so *magnanimous*. He surrounds me in my own *EDEN* and gives me leave to play with all the pretty boys and girls, but it is a *cage*. He sends me doctors to *minister to me* as if *I* were the mad one! I, who only wanted affection, and society, and entertainment, when he couldn't be bothered to show me *any* of those. All of my skills and qualities that I had so assiduously developed — to please, to delight, to *seduce* — and the *fucking prig* could scarcely be *forced* to come to my bed *twice* to father the two brats he showed no interest in siring. MY HUSBAND! Who only wishes to be out and killing things. And when I am bored, or angry, or hungry, or lonely, he sends the doctor to drug me, and poke at me, and give me *strange dreams*." She shuddered, but her fevered eyes remained locked on me. "And you, with your *sweet* husband, who fucks you until you weep, I am sure. Does he tell you he will always love you? Does he tell you that he will always give you everything you need? *HE LIES*. He will cage you, as my husband has caged me, and soon, so soon, you will want to kill yourself or, even better, *KILL HIM!*" And with that, she lunged and attempted to take the shovel from me.

As I said, I am stronger than she — yet her fury gave her frenzied vigor, and I struggled to keep her from tearing the shovel from my grip. I had no doubt that, should she wrench it from me, she would beat me with it, and I had no reason to believe that she would spare me in any way.

We wrestled over the thing for what felt like an eternity — and I have spent many happier eternities. Just as I began to fear that, for all of my country strength, she might win out, there was a loud *crack*. My *great friend*'s eyes rolled back in her head, and she slumped to the ground.

Standing above her was Mrs. Grouse, her stick raised in case the lady stirred again. She did not. "Jumped-up tart," muttered the midwife, and then called out, "*Silas! Come t'us! NOW, boy!*"

I thanked my saviour, asking her how she had come upon us.

"Oh, us could hear tha' shot in t'house and all. Our son should've been here quick-like. *Silas!*"

She knelt, taking a leaf from the ground, and held it before Lady Malkin's mouth. It fluttered there, and the midwife nodded, standing again.

When the gamekeeper finally arrived, breathless, he gaped at the three of us women. "Ma?"

"Th'art a great mutton-head, Silas," Mrs. Grouse sighed. "Did'ee not hear t'gunshot and all?"

"Aye, Ma," said Young Grouse — and I could truly believe he was *Young* Grouse, for he stood before his mother like a child caught filching apples. "Us's over by t'manor. Had to run t'whole way."

"Oh, aye? Well, ay'up then, boy-o. All in good time. Lady Muck there tried t'kill our Mistress Darcy. Us's whacked her good and proper as she deserves." She leaned on her stick and looked down at the crumpled form of Lady Malkin. "Art'ee gonna get yon baggage up and off t'*manor* then, boy-o?"

Astonished, her son nodded.

"Geron w'thee, then."

And so he threw Lady Malkin's limp body over his shoulder like a bagged deer and we followed him back through the woods.

"Should've knowed tha' vixen'd get up to nowt," the old woman sighed. "She's a bad'un, through and through."

When we got to the house, Mr. Reynolds and one of the footmen met us. They took Mr. Grouse's burden from him, and I told them to take her up to one of the guest rooms on the second floor — one far from any drainpipes or trellises.

I told them that Lady Malkin had injured herself, that she was not well, and that we must keep her in the room until I say that she may leave.

Mr. Reynolds looked at me, and at the lady in his arms, no doubt taking in our bruises and the state of our clothing, and, to his great credit, simply answered that it would be done, adding that, as I had clearly intended (though I had not said), Lady Malkin's needs would be seen to in the room, but that she would not be allowed to leave it, since *she might do herself further injury.* He further suggested that I send a letter to Langley Park, since the his lordship's household included a physician who might best look to the lady's needs.

We all nodded, and they took *yon baggage* into the house. I was uneasy, and wished only to lay down there upon the gravel and weep. The struggle with Lady Malkin left me more than overwrought, and the idea of calling for the doctor to *minister* to her made me more than a little nauseated.

Mrs. Grouse reached over, loosed the shovel that I was still carrying from my grip, and said, "Th'ast done well, lass. But th'art not alone. Young Reynolds'll make sure Lady Summat don't do thee harm, nor herself. Get'ee in. Dost need us t'come with'ee?"

"No, thank you, Mrs. Grouse," I said, attempting to stand tall once again. "I do not believe I need trouble you any further. I owe you my life."

"Nay," she answered with a wave of her hand. "'Tis more like *she* owes us — if us hadn't've knocked her silly, thee'd've taken they shovel and bashed'er pretty head in — and good riddance to bad rubbish. Good'en, Mistress Darcy."

"Good evening, Mrs. Grouse." Before she left, I felt compelled to ask her given name, since we are certain to remain in *intimate* contact.

The old woman grinned at me, her grey-green eyes sparkling, and said that, of course, it is *Elizabeth.*

Of course.

And so I informed poor Junkets that after all of my protestations that he should rest until the morning, I must beg him to prepare to carry an urgent letter south this very evening. I will indeed write to Lord Malkin as well, although I do not have the stomach to request that he send his physician — Lady Malkin's cries are echoing still through my very soul and I do not wish to return her to what she sees as *a cage* — though I also do not believe that she can possibly be set free. She is clearly a danger to herself and others.

Oh, Darcy, I have so wished for you to be here these past weeks, and yet now I truly, urgently *need* you here. I have no knowledge of how to handle this business. Should I send someone to fetch the Sheriff? Would doing so put *me* at risk? I have, after all, *lain hands* upon a Countess, and immured her in our house — accommodation that I have no doubt she will deeply resent when she wakes.

I cannot tell *anyone* that it was Mrs. Grouse who rendered her ladyship unconscious — though I will defend to my last breath her choice in doing so. Yet I fear that the Ginivers will scarcely thank her for what she has done.

How can this be carried off without dishonour or further distress?

Oh, Darcy, what am I to do?

Desperately yours,

Elizabeth Anne Bennet Darcy

Aside – A Most Distressing Encounter

From Elizabeth Darcy to August Giniver, Lord Malkin

Pemberley, Derbyshire, *August 27*

My Lord Malkin,

I am writing on a matter of some urgency concerning your wife, and your own health.

While I should prefer to have my husband reach out to your lordship, he is at the moment in London, and so it is left to me. I apologise for writing so without having first had the opportunity meet you in person. Unfortunately, I have had a most distressing encounter with Lady Malkin, which forces me to overstep the dictates of propriety.

I regret to inform you that I came upon Lady Malkin in a state of great agitation, searching through the Pemberley woods for a set of poisonous mushrooms that she and I had been warned of some days ago by Mrs. Grouse, the midwife. I was quite astonished that her ladyship should be undertaking so hazardous an activity — and in our woods. When I confronted her, she made it clear that she intended to use the mushrooms to do away with your lordship or, failing that, herself.

When I attempted to stop her, she laid hands upon me, and one of my people had to restrain her forcibly.

Lady Malkin is currently resting in one of our guest rooms at Pemberley. Once she rises, I fear too greatly for her safety and for yours, my lord, to allow her liberty. I am no legal scholar, and yet her threat against you, against herself, and against myself or anyone who might attempt to stop her seems too real not to be taken seriously. Therefore, my lord, I ask your permission to write the Sheriff so that he may see to this matter.

Once more, I regret not being able to introduce myself to you under more pleasant circumstances.

Your obedient servant,

Elizabeth Darcy

14 – I Ride

From Fitzwilliam Darcy to Elizabeth Darcy

London
August 28

Elizabeth,

I ride.

I pray that I may arrive at Pemberley before Junkets and this letter reach you — I shall ride in fear for your safety, your reassurances (though greatly appreciated) notwithstanding.

That I did not foresee such evil in Elizabeth Giniver (whom I cannot call in any sense *lady*) shames me.

That I have allowed my beloved wife to come so near to mischief horrifies me.

That I may yet in some way help set this right is all that I can think on, and so, as soon as I have handed this letter to Junkets, I will call for my own horses and ride through the night.

Should you receive this before you see me, please, Lizzy, do not *speak* to that person. Do not allow her any courtesy or consideration of person or place. Keep her locked in a secure room until I am there, and have called the Sheriff's bailiffs from Derby and seen her formally charged. She has trespassed on both our property and your person, she has *assaulted* you, and she has clearly shown a willingness to do harm either to her husband, or to herself.

In either case, should she or any other ask, *let this letter serve as a Writ of Indictment and Attainder* that I, in my place as Justice of the Peace for the Crown to the County of Derbyshire, serve upon Elizabeth Giniver, the Countess Malkin, for trespass, assault, and attempted murder, that she may be held until such time as another justice may arraign her and judge her fitness for trial.

My love, I have failed you.

I ride.

Yours,

Fitzwilliam Henry, Darcy by birth
Bennet by God's Good Grace

Aside – Paroxysms

from Thomas Giniver, Lord Malkin, to Elizabeth Darcy

Langley Park
Derbyshire

Aug 28

My Dear Mrs. Darcy,

How lovely of you to reach out to me, my dear! I am terribly sorry for the trouble that Lady Malkin has put you through, and wish to assure you that, whatever her stated intentions, I was almost certainly never in any danger.

I have heard such glowing reports of you from my son and my dear Gussie that I should have looked for some opportunity to make your closer acquaintance in any case. I am delighted that this deuced uncomfortable position in which Lady Malkin has put you has, at the least, given us a chance to make our introductions one to another.

My wife has had episodes of such behaviour on some few occasions over the years. Her physician, Dr. Butler, has diagnosed a rather persistent form of hysteria, and prescribed regular doses of laudanum and the administration of what he terms *hysterical paroxysm*, both of which treatments Lady Malkin seems to enjoy. He also recommends, on the one hand, *regular social stimulation,* but on the other, not so much as may trigger the hysteria. And so I keep Lady Malkin here at Langley Park, in the hope that we might create a pleasant enough situation to discourage her from becoming agitated, while not so stimulating her as to encourage her to fly into hysteria.

I fear that our recent, pleasant in-flow of company, including Mr. Shelley and his peculiar female amanuensis, but also our delightful neighbors, yourself and your sisters, may have tipped her equilibrium so that her condition has got the better of her.

I have sent this letter by Dr. Butler, along with several of our largest groomsmen, so that they may convey Lady Malkin back to our home, where the good doctor may treat her affliction and return her to her usual, charming self.

On those occasions in the past when she has threatened mischief upon my person or upon her own, a few weeks of *treatment* have been all that was needed to render her no longer any threat to herself or anyone else.

All of this is, I fear, my own fault. My good friend Henry Darcy, your husband's late father, used to laugh that my beautiful and vivacious wife should be married to someone so ill-prepared to enjoy her charms. He used to call me *Menelaus*, which I must admit was apt, since while I do care deeply for Lady Malkin, it is true that I have not perhaps been the husband for whom she might have wished. I therefore consider it my duty to provide her with what help I can.

I must ask that you *not* contact the Sheriff, since, as you see, this is a matter not for *Justitia*, but rather for *Hygeia*. I apologise for any discomfort that Lady Malkin may have caused you and shall make it good in any way that you ask, but I must stipulate that you not bring this matter to the courts, for I fear that Lady Malkin's *hysteria* would undoubtedly worsen in such distressing, insalubrious circumstances.

I do recognise that I am asking a rather large favour of you.

Yet I have, as I say, heard such reports of your intelligence and kindness from my children that I trust that my request shall be met with compassion and acquiescence.

In the mean time, my son has come to me to ask my permission that he court your sister, Miss Catherine Bennet. While I have not met the girl, my son himself reports her to be a charming and spirited creature, reports that his sister Gussie echoes. They tell me that your father is a gentleman from Hertfordshire, where I spent some time in my youth on one of our family's estates, since it was closer to my school. I have very fond memories of my time in the county, playing a game with the local children that I believe was called *Tom of Straw*.

In any case, I have given my son permission to court Miss Bennet. Gussie warns me that she is not certain what kind of settlement your sister might bring with her, yet I have long wished that my son find a bride whose company he actually enjoys. For some time, I held out some hope that he and Miss Darcy would find an understanding. However, they have both made it quite clear that this shall not happen, and so I am pleased that my son should be so taken with your sister. He speaks highly of her *exuberance* and her *good humor,* and Gussie tells me she is not only very *pretty* but quite good with *languages.* I hope that she may be prevailed upon to look kindly upon so *un-exuberant* a creature as my son.

I should be delighted to have you, your husband, and your sisters join us here at Langley once young Mr. Darcy returns from the City. I should love to take him hunting, although I know that he feels somewhat ill at ease in my presence — I assume that this is because of my wife taking him as a lover when they were both quite young. Please assure your husband that I hold him in no disapprobation, and that, indeed, I appreciate his having aided Lady Malkin with her *paroxysms.*

Again, I am pleased to have made your acquaintance and look forward to many years of continued and pleasant social intercourse between our families.

Yours truly, &c.,

August Giniver

12th Earl Malkin, Graf von Löwenhau, Baronet of Badequelle & Welwyn, &c.

Aside – Marital Arrangements

From Jane Bingley to Elizabeth Darcy

Grosvener St, London, *Aug. 29*

My dearest Lizzy,

We were very much looking forward to seeing your husband again once we reached London; however we have just visited the house on Berkeley Square and were told that he had left post-haste for Pemberley yesterday morning. While the housekeeper assured us that all was well, I hope you will understand that Charles and I were both somewhat alarmed to find that he had left so suddenly, and without leaving any word for us. I hope that all is indeed well, there? I hope that you have not found yourself ill; the rain when we left Charles's family in Cheshire seemed little conducive to good health, and I know how you love to be abroad, even in inclement weather. If you are unwell, please do let me know, and I shall be there as soon as a carriage can bear me.

We enjoyed our return to Netherfield, where my new sister Caroline continues to keep the house so well. She has shown nothing but kindness and consideration since our wedding, and so I am now inclined to dismiss any lingering suspicion as to her intentions. Indeed, I feel most sorry that she finds herself with no immediate prospects (though I am of course not at all sorry that her most desired prospect is no longer available). Our father and mother were very welcome guests at the hall, and we at Longbourn. I will grant, however, that Mama's rather persistent enquiries as to the cost of various furnishings (no less than about the arrival of my *monthly visitor*, which she wished to discuss *at the table*) made both Charles and me somewhat uncomfortable, as I am sure you can imagine. However, if we left Hertfordshire some days more quickly than we had intended, please do not think that it was in any way *not desirable* to stay longer because of Mama's questions (nor uncle Phillips's attempts to solicit employment). Rather, we were very excited to travel on to London, and likewise excited to see your wonderful husband. Our own disappointment, then, was added to our alarm, dearest Lizzy, when we found that he had flown back north.

As I have mentioned, my *visitor* did indeed arrive at about its usual time, just as we returned to Hertfordshire. I found that I was most disappointed, too, at its arrival. Has yours come? I have the hope, as I've told you, that when I am blessed with child, you shall be too; that we should share that experience as we have shared so much else. Yet if you are now so blessed, it should of course make me more happy than I can say.

By the way, I received from our aunt Gardiner a letter some week or so after the weddings. As always, it was full of her wisdom and good humour. However, she did make some suggestions of marital *arrangements* that I find that I scarcely know how to read. Did she send such a letter to you, dearest Lizzy? And if she did, were you able to *apply* any of her suggestions? In either case, I should love your advice in this matter, for I know that you are far less flustered by such things than I, and may perhaps assist me in becoming a better wife — and, if I understand our aunt correctly, a happier one.

Not that I have any cause to complain of unhappiness, as you know! Oh, Lizzy, how is it that we should both have been delivered every possible source of happiness — excepting of course to live closer to one another? I have never thought myself a particularly happy, fortunate, nor deserving woman, yet I find not only that I have been showered in all the felicity for which I might have wished, but that my most beloved sister has been showered with the the same. I miss you, and hope that we shall see each other again soon. Please do write and assure me that you are well, and all is well, and all manner of things shall be well.

Yours, &c.

Jane Bingley

PS I have just received a letter from Kitty, who tells me that you have made the acquaintance of some *quite interesting* neighbors. She seems very enthusiastic about them, though she shares little more detail. Can you tell me more of what has so excited her?

Epilogue – Journeys End in Lovers Meeting

Pemberley, Derbyshire

He had ridden three horses out from under him, and yet he had not been able to stop or to rest — not even when he found himself almost dropping from the saddle.

Elizabeth was in danger. That was his only thought. He must return as quickly as possible.

As his sweat-foamed mount staggered up the long, long drive to Pemberley, he could not feel hope, could not feel relief — not until he held his wife in his arms.

Young Clarke, the footman, stood waiting at the top of the drive, doing his best not to look astonished to see his master arriving in so disheveled a state.

"Your mistress?" Darcy rasped as he slid to the ground and let the groom take the horse.

"On the veranda with the young ladies," Clarke answered.

Darcy thanked him and strode into the house as quickly as his unsteady legs would allow.

Mrs. Reynolds met him in the front hall, carrying a glass of some sweet, lemon-flavoured beverage, which he happily gulped down. She then handed him a damp cloth, which he used to wipe his face. Mr. Reynolds opened the door out into the garden, where —

Where Elizabeth stood, whole, unharmed, and utterly beautiful.

He meant to say all sorts of very heartfelt things about how he would protect her, how he would take care of everything, how he would never leave her alone again.

He said none of these things. Instead, he threw his arms around her and wept.

———

She ran a finger over his chest, trailing his sweat in patterns that he wished he could see. Her voice low, as he only heard it in such moments of intimacy, she sighed, *"Full nakedness! All joys are due to thee. As souls unbodied, bodies uncloth'd must be."*

He shivered at the pleasure of the slide of her flesh on his flesh. All he could do was hum in agreement.

"So," she laughed, "do you trust now that I am unhurt and hale?"

"Indeed," he murmured. "I have examined you fully and found no flaw. I feel more than a bit a fool for having ridden to no purpose."

"Not to no purpose!" She kissed his neck. "I have wished you here for *days*, and here you are!"

"Here I am," he agreed, smiling. His legs were sore, his back ached, and yet he could not remember ever feeling better. "I am so glad to have granted your wish." He ran his fingers through her curls, which had fallen from the neat bun atop her head and flowed down her back and cheek.

"Do you like my hair?" she asked.

"I do."

"Hmm. As I love yours." She reached up and ran a finger through his own dark, slick locks. Her voice took on a mischievous edge. "Hmm. Even so, I have grown rather fond of Augustina and Tommy's as well. Perhaps we shall have a *ginger swot* of our own?"

"Ah, Lizzy," he laughed, "unless you play me foul, which I know you would never do, I do not think that a couple who have come from a line so sable-haired as mine and so wood-brown as yours could produce a child with locks as flaming as Augustina's."

She laughed too, and slid up to kiss his ear.

However, thoughts of Augustina's parentage brought him in mind once again of Augustina's mother. He put his arms around his wife and stilled her. "Lizzy, was Lady Malkin greatly upset when the doctor came?"

His wife sighed and tucked her face beneath his chin. "She was... not happy. Once she woke, she railed quite a bit — she did considerable damage to the room, but Mr. Reynolds made sure she did not escape. Florry tells me that you could hear some of her howls from the attic. I fear she will be tarred with the label of *madwoman* for some time."

"She *is* mad."

"Yes. But however mad she may have been to begin with — and from Lord Malkin's letter I believe she may have been for quite some time — I cannot help but feel that I have done her more harm than good."

"Yet she went with Dr. Butler?" He did not wish to be having this conversation — he wished to be loving his wife. And yet this was troubling her, and he felt he must listen.

"As meek as a lamb," sighed Elizabeth. "Yet I know that she expressed loathing for the doctor and his *treatment,* for all that Lord Malkin said that she *enjoyed* it."

"Then we must leave her to the doctor's care, my love. For she was not in her right mind when you met her in the wood."

"Clearly not."

"Then absolve yourself, Elizabeth. You have acted for the general good. You could not have helped her in any better way."

"Hmm." She slid up, her whole body pressing on his, and kissed him, and sore, tired, and aching though he may have been, he truly felt beyond wonderful. With her teeth, she nipped at his lip. "So, my dearest Darcy, what would you say to a long, hot, leisurely bath?"

"I should say, my dearest Mrs. Darcy, that that sounds like a truly marvelous suggestion." And so he sat up and cradled his *uncloth'd* wife in his arms, standing from the bed with the intent of getting them both clothed — but only until the servants had filled the large tub behind the screen in the corner of the room.

As he carried her toward where their dressing gowns were hung, the door flew open, and in strode a dirty, road-worn Junkets, holding before him the very letter that Darcy had put into his hands the day before. Junkets's eyes flew wide as he saw what he had interrupted, and he looked quickly down to the floor. "Erm… Letter for you, Mrs. Darcy… from… Mr. Darcy?"

Elizabeth laughed, attempting to hide herself against him, and leaving Darcy to answer. "Thank you, John. Leave it on the table there. Then go and get yourself some food and rest."

Gaze still averted, Junkets deposited the letter where directed and began to leave, but Darcy stopped him. "Oh — and Mr. Keats, if you could let Mrs. Reynolds know that we require hot water for a bath, we should greatly appreciate it."

Postscript – By the Horns

From Elizabeth Darcy to Margaret Gardiner

Pemberley, Derbyshire, *September 2*

My dearest aunt Margaret,

Such a to-do met your letter upon its arrival in this evening's post!

Kitty, as you may have heard, has acquired an admirer — one Thomas Giniver, whose father, as it happens, is August Giniver, the 12th Earl Malkin, et cetaera, whom you probably remember hearing of from your time here in Derbyshire. Well, young Master Giniver has written Papa to beg his permission — not to ask for Kitty's hand, but to *court* her.

Papa, who wrote me, is wildly amused, as one would expect, and told me that he granted the boy permission to pass the time with his daughter — since *the boy* was clearly going to do so whether Papa said yay or nay.

Mama, on the other hand, seems to have been overcome by mother-quakes of mixed maternal delight and anxiety. She sent Kitty a letter that arrived in the morning post (while yours arrived in the evening): it was apparently stuffed with advice of what Kitty should and shouldn't do, and why it would be disastrous were Kitty to fail to *grasp the bull by the horns* and *land the fish* (my mother's mixing of metaphors can at the least always be counted upon to provide some entertainment). Poor Kitty was so overcome by the letter that she retreated to her bed and has scarcely left it all day. It will not surprise you, then, that when Master Giniver and his sister appeared this afternoon (as they have often done these past weeks) and Georgiana and I had to tell them that Kitty was *not well,* Thomas was quite solicitous in asking after her. But of course his presence was precisely what Kitty *did not* wish.

And so it was only after they left that we were graced once again by my sister's presence — still with swollen eyes and tear-streaked cheeks, but at least among us. Georgiana was very sympathetic and solicitous toward Kitty, which was good, since I only wanted to laugh.

Now, I am astonished to find that I believe that, whether or not Thomas Giniver be a proper match for my sister (and despite his birth there are things about him that certainly make Darcy and me question that premise), he and Kitty seem genuinely fond of each other. In addition, Kitty has displayed a previously unsuspected air of command with the young lord, and he seems very much to like it. As my husband pointed out once he had seen the young couple together, they are certainly no worse matched than he and I would have appeared to be when we first met.

That being the case, I believe that all my mother has managed to do in writing Kitty is to take her own agitation at the prospect of her youngest unwed daughter possibly marrying the heir to a peer, and to pour it like so much boiling fat from a roasting pan into that very daughter, where it has, naturally, caught fire. I have not seen Kitty look so distraught — not even when Lydia got to go to Brighton without her. We can hope and trust that this occasion will end better than that, yet in the meantime, Kitty has remained on the edge of tears, with poor, sweet Georgiana following her about with a handkerchief (as with a closed umbrella), waiting for the next outpouring.

It was into this happy scene that the maid arrived with your letter.

Thank you once more for your very helpful suggestions — and in this case, I speak of the ones intended for implementation *outside* of the bed chamber. You are quite right — I must trust my husband. Indeed, I have no real choice but to trust him, yet it is, as you clearly know, terribly hard. It is a good thing that I love him so, and that he is so handsome.

And speaking of his sable-haired beauty, I have in fact learned the secret that I feared he was keeping from me: it seems that he was worried that the lady with whom he had first shared intimacy (and I *do* mean of a carnal nature) had got a child by him.

Now, if I were to tell you that the lady herself has the kind of extremely fair hair that is sometimes referred to as *flaxen*, that the woman's husband comes from a long line of redheads, and that the child in question bears a head of equally remarkable, sunset red hair, how should you have answered my black-haired husband, if he had shared his fears with you?

I can tell you how I responded: with outright, unchecked laughter.

Poor Darcy. I know he was relieved when I pointed out the unlikelihood of his having had any part in fathering the child — but I believe that I hurt his pride as well.

Nonetheless, we have both undertaken to follow your commandment to love and trust one another, so long as we both shall live.

I do indeed have a wonderful husband; whether he have a wonderful wife remains to be seen, but I shall do my best.

And of course, thank you too for the *other,* more acrobatic suggestion, which, as it happens, my husband and I had already discussed in our letters and put into practice this very morning *inside* the bed chamber. You are as always quite correct — it was *most* mutually enjoyable. You are right yet again — I do not wish to imagine you and uncle Edward engaged in anything like such an exchange.

Even so, I promise to provide sweet Joan with all of the benefits of my experience (as enhanced by you) in that distant future when she shall need it. My own scruples be hanged — I know that once my cousins need the knowledge, they shall appreciate it, and so I shall provide it.

Of course, the idea of Joan or of young Freddie taking a husband is more than a bit breathtaking. Yet Joan is but a decade Kitty's junior, and indeed my bunny subjects shall be greatly relieved once Alfreda takes an interest in suitors rather than in terrorizing them.

There was another, rather unpleasant to-do that rather disturbed the peace of this idyllic Arcadia some days ago, and has upset my own peace more than I should like to admit. I was forced to halt a local woman in her intent to harm her husband or, failing that, herself. I do not regret stopping her, not at all. She was clearly insane, and a danger to herself and others.

Even in Paradise, there am I, sayeth Death.

Yet I have been quite unhappy at my own involvement in the affair. For I cannot help but feel that in allowing her to be released to her husband's care I have returned the poor woman to a prison that does damage to her very soul.

The only positive thing to come out of the whole business was that Darcy flew back home, alarmed that I had been even momentarily in danger myself. And so it was that we were able to put your *store of wifely knowledge* to further use.

He tells me that I must not blame myself for the woman's unhappiness — that she brought that upon herself, to the extent that she was at all responsible for her own actions. Yet I cannot help but question my own culpability in the matter.

It does not help that the woman is a neighbor, and one with whom I shall have to interact — as with her husband. I do not know how to speak with them. Yet the husband has invited all of us to dine at their house. Which would be more awkward and unpleasant: to go, or not to go?

That is the question.

On the subject of pertinent questions, my dear aunt Margaret, were you aware of the *surprise* that our husbands prepared for me?

They have invested in a certain printing house in Fleet Street, one that specialises in the publication of poetry.

I suppose that we are *both* now partners in one of my favourite publishers, and one whose books you and I have shared with pleasure on a number of occasions.

This does not seem like the sort of *gift* I should have expected from uncle Edward, however expansive he may have been feeling. And while it is precisely the sort of gesture I should expect from my husband, I am quite certain our intimacy is not yet well enough established for him to know my reading habits *so* thoroughly.

And so I ask again, were you aware of this *surprise,* which delighted me more than I can possibly say? And, if so, did you (as I strongly suspect) suggest the investment to my husband?

If so, I thank you. You already know that I love you dearly, but if this was your doing — and even if it was not — I must tell you so again.

It is raining here in Derbyshire. I hope that it has at least cooled somewhat there in the city. *When the snows come,* as it happens, we may have reason to visit you, for my new sister Georgiana (who asks to be remembered to you) is tentatively considering enduring *the Season* in London. If so, then we shall see you sooner than I might have hoped, for while I should miss the promised snowy weather (I can only imagine the glories of Pemberley in winter), we should be able to see each other, which should make up for any loss.

Please give my love to my uncle and to my cousins. Tell Freddie that I shall speak with the bunnies, but that they are a proud race, and not easily persuaded to leave their ancestral lands. And do *not* tell Joan of the letters that I shall write her when her time comes to marry. I do not think that she would find that news welcome just yet — though I welcome *all* news (and further *suggestions*) from you, beloved aunt.

Your loving niece,

Elizabeth Darcy
1ˢᵗ of that name, Mistress of Pemberley, Queen of the Derbyshire Bunnies, et cetaera

– Fin–

The Pemberley Letters, vol. 1

Author's Note

Thank you for reading this game of literary *Tom-'o-Straw!* I have had a wonderful time playing in the fields first planted by Jane Austen, and I hope that you have enjoyed playing along with me.

If you did, please do let your friends know! We authors do our best to delight and entertain, and when we manage actually to do so, we count on our readers to let us know that we've done well (or even when we haven't) — but we also count on you to spread the word. Old-fashioned word of mouth is of course always delightful — the best medium for all communication, I think — but if you happen to be connected to the world via Augustina's *electrical ether,* then please consider visiting **stillpointdigital.com/book/darcy-and-desire** and sharing with your friends, &c.

This is intended to be the first in a series of books tracing Elizabeth and Darcy's correspondence through the months and years follow-ing their *happily ever after.* If you wish to hear about my up-coming books, events, giveaways, and a great deal of other news, do sign up at **stillpointdigital.com/aphrodite/news.**

—

The path to this book's publication has been more than usually circuitous and serendipitous.

It started as a birthday gift.

I wrote the first letter as a present for a young friend, who went by the handle **kit_ana**, who had asked for a steamy bit of Lizzy/Darcy fun. I combined that with a small reference to another of my favorite works of genius set in Napoleonic-era Derbyshire. I was very pleased with the piece, and had no further plans for it — until many, many years later, Mr. Darcy came knocking on my door and asked if he should not have the privilege of answering his wife's letter. Once he had done so, Lizzy (being Lizzy) couldn't wait quite so long... and soon I had the beginnings of the whole correspondence taking shape.

The plot began to reveal itself very organically. The Ginivers, who had initially been inspired by that other Regency-period work I mentioned, began to take on their own shape and character, offering me fascinating possibiliities to explore Austen's characters and her world. What had started as a crossover piece of fanfiction, if you will, now became firmly set in Austen's Regency garden — but soon became populated by historical literary characters as well.

It may not surprise you to read that I have my own very strong opinions about English literature in general, and about the Romantics in particular. If you disagree with my portrayal of them and of their writing here, I apologize for the offense — but for the opinions, not at all.

The setting of this book in time I have had to leave purposefully a bit vague — the action takes place (more or less) during the summer of 1814. While you wouldn't know it from these letters (any more than from the pages of Austen's novels), Napoleon has just been defeated (for the first time) and sent into exile on the isle of Elba. England was breathing a sigh of relief (although they were still fighting in North America.) While I know that this is later than most scholars would have suggested for the final scenes of *Pride & Prejudice* (which was, after all, published the year before!), it works for the lives of the three wonderful writers who appear in these pages — the Shelleys and John Keats. As for those characters... please consider the portrayals here to be pure fiction in service of this particular story. I have attempted to draw them as true to the historical record as I could; however, I will allow that the needs of the story (and my own prejudices, perhaps) have colored the way they've appeared here.

I still agree with Elizabeth about Shelley being *a bit of a cad*, however.

Regarding Lady Malkin's... *treatment*. Women's "hysteria" (which is to say, anything from rage and frustration to actual mental illness) was in fact treated during the early nineteenth century through a combination of laudanum (tincture of opium) and "hysterical paroxysms" (manual — and frequently involuntary — stimulation to orgasm). That this "treatment" was less than effective in "curing" the "patient" might not surprise us today. It seems a gross, barbaric mistreatment of those women; however, it was in fact an accepted medical practice of the day. It shouldn't be a surprise, then, that Lady Malkin identified with Madame de Merteuil, who raged at the constrictions laid upon her by her sex and station.

And Tom-o'-Straw? I made it up, based on a variety of games of tag that we used to play when I was young. But I kind of want to find a scarecrow and go play now. What do you think?

—

*I*f it takes a village to raise a child, it clearly takes an army to write a book. There are many, many folks I need to thank, beginning with you, since you're still reading!

Several communities of online readers helped me to fashion this series of letters into what I hope and trust is a coherent novel. On Discord, HazzaP helped me keep Nanny Grouse intelligible and (hopefully) correct, and GriffindorHealer, deadwoodpecker, and Dragyn42 all provided wonderful feedback. On AO3, I received invaluable comments and suggestions from an enormous group of wonderful author/readers, including BrytteMystere, DonOsservatore (for asking many, many questions), Search-Find-Read (for making me be absolutely sure about the red hair thing), Ms_Pimprenelle (for showing me the truth about the Gardiners' names), Russako, fanartyparty (for being as big a fan of Mrs. Gardiner as I am), legionofthebeast, and many, many more.

Thank you to my publisher, David Kudler, who has served as first editor for this as on all my books — and for being the voice of Mr. Darcy on the audiobook as well! Thanks to the delightful, talented narrator Ella Lynch for bringing Lizzy so delightfully to life.

And thank you, as always, to M, without whom none of this would have been possible, or worth doing.

Characters

NB: Those characters who appear in **Pride & Prejudice** *or who are based on historical figures are set in* **boldface.**

At Pemberley:

Elizabeth "Lizzy" Anne Darcy, née Bennet (22)

Catherine "Kitty" Bennet (18 — Lizzy's younger sister; fourth of the Bennet daughters)

Georgiana Darcy (16 — Darcy's younger sister and ward)

Mrs. Annesly (companion to Georgiana; visiting brother & sister-in-law)

Mrs. Reynolds (Houskeeper at Pemberley)

Mr. Reynolds (Butler at Pemberley)

Mary Patchett (Cook at Pemberley)

Frances "Fanny" Lewis (Scullery maid at Pemberley; soon to be married)

Florence "Florry" Gwynn (Lady's maid to Lizzy; niece to "Young" Grouse)

Anne "Annie" Gwynn (Farmer's wife; mother to Florry; sister to "Young" Grouse)

Silas "Young" Grouse (Gamekeeper for Pemberley)

Esau "Old" Grouse (Former gamekeeper for Pemberley)

Elizabeth "Nanny" or "Mother" Grouse (Wife of "Old" Grouse, healer and midwife)

At Langley Park:

Elizabeth "Liesel" Giniver, née Desmond, the Countess Malkin (36 — Wife of Lord Malkin; daughter of an Austrian noblewoman and a wealthy London merchant; mother of Thomas and Augustina)

Augustus Giniver, 12th Earl Malkin, &c. (62 — Husband of Lady Malkin, father of Thomas and Augustina; friend of the late Mr. Darcy)

Thomas Giniver (17 — Older brother of Augustina)

Augustina Giniver (16 — Younger sister of Thomas)

Septimus Lackey (28 — Augustina's tutor)

Percy Byshe Shelley (28 — Renowned poet)

Mary Wollstonecraft Godwin (17 — Daughter of two famous authors; soon to be Mrs. Shelley and the author of *Frankenstein*)

London (12, Berkeley Square):

Fitzwilliam Henry Darcy (28 — Husband to Lizzy, brother to Georgiana)

Harrison (Darcy's valet)

Starkey (Darcy's driver)

Mrs. Martin (Housekeeper)

Mrs. McCartney (Cook)

Mr. Kite (Darcy's factor or business agent)

John "Junkets" Keats (19 — Cockney, poet, apothocary, and courier)

Edward Gardiner (38 — Brother to Lizzy's mother, uncle to Bennets)

Margaret Gardiner (34 —Wife to Edward, aunt to Bennets)

Joan Gardiner (9 — Lizzy's eldest cousin)

Alfreda "Freddie" Gardiner (7 — Lizzy's second oldest cousin)

William "Billy" Gardiner (5 — Lizzy's third eldest cousin)

Edward "Eddie" Gardiner, Jr. (3 — Lizzy's youngest cousin)

Jane Bingley, née Bennet (23 — Lizzy's eldest sister)

Charles Bingley (27 — Jane's husband and Darcy's best friend)

About the Author

CADY WEST is the Regency romance pen name for **K.D. WEST,** a bestselling author of contemporary, fantasy, and (very) steamy romance. Cady/K.D. is also a performer and teacher who lives in a small suburb of a large city, has always loved Jane Austen's books and characters, and feels like a kid in a candy shop, having the opportunity to play in her garden.

Darcy & Desire is the first novel in the forthcoming series, The Pemberley Letters. This collection of witty, entertaining, and frankly sexy correspondence explores between one of literature's most beloved couples in the months and years following their *happily ever after.*

For more, follow at **stillpointdigital.com/aphrodite/new**s, at **kdwestwrites.wordpress.com**, or at **stillpointeros.com/kdwest**

Twitter: @kdwestwrites
Instagram: @kdwestwrites
Facebook page: kdwestauthor

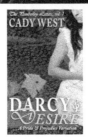

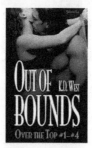

CPSIA information can be obtained
at www.ICGtesting.com
Printed in the USA
BVHW031713060521
606648BV00006B/879